Walking Ivy's Path

WALKING IVY'S PATH

Stella Cooper Mitchell

iUniverse, Inc.
New York Lincoln Shanghai

Walking Ivy's Path

Copyright © 2006 by Stella Cooper Mitchell

All rights reserved. No part of this book may be used or reproduced by any means, graphic, electronic, or mechanical, including photocopying, recording, taping or by any information storage retrieval system without the written permission of the publisher except in the case of brief quotations embodied in critical articles and reviews.

iUniverse books may be ordered through booksellers or by contacting:

iUniverse
2021 Pine Lake Road, Suite 100
Lincoln, NE 68512
www.iuniverse.com
1-800-Authors (1-800-288-4677)

This book is a work of fiction. Names, characters, places and incidents are products of the author's imagination or are used fictitiously. Any resemblance to actual events or locales or persons, living or dead, is entirely coincidental.

Cover design by Michael Dyson

ISBN-13: 978-0-595-38920-9 (pbk)
ISBN-13: 978-0-595-83298-9 (ebk)
ISBN-10: 0-595-38920-1 (pbk)
ISBN-10: 0-595-83298-9 (ebk)

Printed in the United States of America

For Jim, Bill and Janice

Chapter 1

Life with George

I was eight years old when I first met George Washington. George and I were in Mama's class, and we never said one word to each other that whole year. One day, Mama invited him to our house to work on a class project. I was horrified!

George was the most God-awful looking child I had ever seen. He was scrawny, with huge teeth and fuzz instead of hair. He had pitiful looking clothes, but they were always starched and ironed. His shoes were too big. They were hand-me-downs from old Dan, I guess.

I wasn't that much cuter myself. I was as fat as a little pig. My Mammie (Mama's mother) had fed me too much good food. My hair was bright red and kinky. I didn't have any friends because I couldn't stand to be around the stupid jerks in our class.

George was so happy to be invited to Mama's house that he ran all the way. He got there before we did.

In those days, we never locked the door. He waited and waited for us, but soon curiosity got the better of him and he started prowling around the house.

He went into my room and started looking in my closet. Maybe he had never seen satin before…I don't know…but he found my satin dress with ivy embroidered on the front. He loved the way it felt, and tried it on. That's when we walked in. There stood George in my best dress. At that moment, I hated George Washington. I started throwing a fit. "Take it off, take it off," I screamed. Mama gave George a big lecture about boys wearing girls' clothes and that it was not normal.

As George took the dress off, his pants leg pulled up and we saw the biggest bruise. Mama said, "George, what happened to your leg?"

"Old Dan kicked me," he said. "He did it when he was drunk. He says he wants to make a man out of me."

Mama was on the phone in two seconds. "Get the law over here, now," she said. In ten minutes the sheriff was knocking on the door.

"Look at this," she said and pulled up George's britches leg.

"Tell them what happened, George." George told the whole story again.

The sheriff wasn't impressed. Child abuse didn't have a name back then.

"A man's got a right to discipline his son," he said.

"You mean you're not going to do anything?" asked Mama. "If you can't do anything, I sure can," she said. "Get in the car, children."

We got in, and she sped off to George's house. She stopped the car, and we got out.

She stormed in the house, and there sat old Dan on the couch, drinking whiskey. She went straight over and kicked the shit out of him.

"What in the hell are you doing, woman?"

"I'm making a man out of you, you son of a bitch," said Mama.

Mama was bigger than old Dan. I guess he knew better than make her any madder than she already was, so he just sat there.

"Get your clothes, George," said Mama. George and I got his pitiful stuff and put it in a paper bag. Old Dan just sat there.

"Get in the car," she said. We did.

That's how George and I became friends. George moved in with us and he never left.

It worked out really well. George and I became as thick as molasses. George could cook, George could clean, and George could iron. Mama and I started eating right. No more Chef Boy Ardé and no more canned chili for us!

Chapter 2

Nettie

George always used a recipe when he cooked...not like Mammie, who fried everything. Mama and I lived with Mammie and Pappy, her parents, until we got our own house.

We moved from Mammie's and Pappy's farm to town. I loved town. Now that I had my friend George, and I was slimming down, my life was showing great improvement.

There were still a few things that needed taking care of. One was Nettie. Nettie lived close to Mammie and Pappy. Mama took us to see Mammie about once a month. Mammie thought she was being sweet, so she would invite Nettie up to play.

George and I always had to play what Nettie wanted to play. Nettie called George "prissy". Nettie pushed me when I wasn't paying attention. Nettie made life hell for George and me. We both hated Nettie.

We didn't like to visit Mammie because we knew Nettie would be there.

"Hurry up," Mama would say, "we're going to Mammie's house."

"No," George and I both said.

"Why not?" asked Mama.

"Nettie'll be there," I said.

"Well, you have to learn how to get along with other people," said Mama.

"Nettie's too mean," said George.

Mama always won, and we went to Mammie's house.

Sure enough, Nettie was already there when we drove up. She immediately smacked George with a mud ball and got his clothes dirty. George thought cleanliness was next to Godliness. He really hated to get dirty, so this really upset him.

"Come on, George and Nettie, let's go play school," I said.

"I don't want to play school," said Nettie. "I want to catch tadpoles in the creek. I'll hit you with another mud ball if you don't." George and I knew we might as well do what she said, or she would terrorize us all day.

The summers in Tennessee were so hot, and the cold creek felt so good on my feet. I tucked my dress tail under the elastic of my bloomer legs. This made my already chubby hips look about twice as big.

"You're so fat," said Nettie.

"And you're so stupid," I said.

We caught a few tadpoles and put them in our bucket. Then we watched skating bugs glide across the water.

"Jesus and skating bugs are the only two things that I know of that can walk on water," said George.

Nettie pushed me in the back and said, "Ivy can."

I fell down in the creek and got my dress and bloomers soaking wet.

Mammie called us to the house and I got scolded for being wet. Nettie lied and said I was clumsy and fell down.

Mammie was baking tea cakes for us, and she just "pooh-poohed" what we said about Nettie.

Nettie got away with being mean one more time.

Chapter 3

Sweet Dumpling

I know Mammie didn't mean to do this to me, but she did. It was a traumatic event that would plague me for a long time.

When the tea cakes were done, Mammie said, "George, Sweet Dumpling, and Nettie…come on in and have some tea cakes."

"Sweet Dumpling, Sweet Dumpling," Nettie screamed and pushed me.

Well, my life was over. Nettie told everybody. They thought that was the funniest thing they had ever heard. My name was "Sweet Dumpling" for the longest time after that. I knew I had to get even.

It took George and me forever, but we finally got our chance. Nettie visited us at Mammie's one day when the road workers were paving the road. We said, "Nettie, let's go watch them work on the road." We stood back, but we told Nettie we would let her stand close to the road so she could see better.

Well, she did. She was very engrossed in the road building and she didn't pay attention to what was happening. A truck came along and a tire hit a pothole. Nettie got covered from head to toe in tar. Only her eyes were the right color. We laughed so hard that I almost peed in my britches, and George was rolling on the ground.

Nettie's mama couldn't get the tar out of Nettie's hair, so she had to shave her head.

George and I called her "Turnip Head" after that. She wasn't too happy about that name, but it stuck with her, just like the tar.

Chapter 4

▼

How George Got His Name

We had Turnip Head Nettie and Sweet Dumpling in our class, so I asked George how he had such an impressive name.

He said that old Dan was half drunk when he got George out of the hospital. Old Dan called a cab to come and take them home because he was too drunk to drive. The cab driver asked, "What's the baby's name?" Old Dan said he didn't know, but about that time they drove by a sign that said "George Washington Insurance Company".

"I think I'll name this boy George Washington," said old Dan.

"That's a fine name," said the cab driver.

"Well, so it is," said old Dan. And that's how George got his name.

I asked Mama to drive George and me around and find the sign. She did, and sure enough, there it was. I'm so glad old Dan looked out the window when he did because the next sign said "Dairy Queen."

I'm so thankful George wasn't named Dairy Queen. I had enough trouble defending George Washington. The children in our class teased him a lot. A few said he was showing off and acting like a big shot. They said he wasn't even George Washington; George Washington was the governor or something like that.

Mama about had a stroke over that statement. "George Washington was our first president," she said. And she said that our George had a lot to live up to. She went on to say, "Our George will be great one day when he's grown up."

George was grinning from ear to ear, like a mule eating sawbriars.

"I won't let you down, Mama!"

Chapter 5

Hog Killing

Every winter, when it got cold enough and the moon was right, we would have to go to Mammie's and Pappy's house to help with hog killing.

Hog killing day was one of the worst days of my life. First of all, I felt so sorry for the hog. There he stood, fat and happy. "Oink, oink." He would look Pappy straight in the eye. Then *Boom*...he was shot straight between the eye! Then he was stuck in the neck with a big knife. After that, he was hung in a tree by his back feet and slit open from his tail to his throat.

George loved hog killing, even though he kept himself sparkling clean all the time. He was the prissiest boy I had ever known.

When the hog was gutted, George would dissect each part of the innards. "Look Ivy, this is the heart," he said, as he cut it open with a butcher knife. Blood squirted all over George. "The heart's got four chambers."

"Leave me alone," I said. "I think I'm going to be sick." The smell of blood and hog intestines was nauseating to me.

"You need to know this for science class," George said.

"I don't want to," I said.

At last, I was saved!

"Young'uns, go to the spring and get us some more water to boil," Pappy said. George and I got a bucket and headed for the spring.

Mammie and Pappy lived way out in the country. Cars rarely passed by. When they did, somebody would yell, "Car coming! Car coming!" They knew everybody who drove up and down the road.

We had to cross the road to get to the spring. "Car coming," said George. So we stopped.

The car passed, and we didn't recognize the stranger driving it. As soon as he passed us, he slammed on the brakes and backed up. He stopped the car, jumped out, grabbed George Washington, put him in the car, and sped off.

I didn't really believe in the booger man, but Mammie threatened me with him when I wouldn't do what she said. "If you don't act right, the booger man will get you," she would say.

I ran screaming to the house. "The booger man got George, the booger man got George."

"What are you talking about?" asked Pappy.

"A stranger in a car stole George," I said.

Pappy stopped rendering lard. "Stop that lying," he said.

"I'm not lying," I said.

Pappy started hollering. "George, George Washington! George, if you don't come here this minute, I'm going to tan your hide!"

Neither George nor I had ever got our hide tanned, but both of us were afraid we might. When we had pushed our luck to the hide tanning stage, we would do what Pappy said.

Pappy kept hollering and running around, looking for George. Finally, he had to go back to the house and tell Mama and Mammie that George had been kidnapped.

Mammie was screaming and wringing her hands. "Oh, Lord, have mercy, save that child!" Mama was on the phone calling the sheriff.

In the meantime, George was in the car with the stranger, and he was scared to death. He started screaming and crying. The more he screamed, the faster the stranger drove, and this scared George even more. Tears and hog blood mixed together, running down George's face.

"Oh Lord, let me save this child before he bleeds to death," the man prayed aloud. "Son, what's your name?" the stranger asked.

"George Washington," George said.

"Oh Lord, it's worse than I thought," the stranger said aloud. "He's talking out of his head." At this point, George was near hysterics.

"Thank you Lord!" the stranger prayed, when he saw the lights of town.

George was trying to explain about hog killing, but the stranger wouldn't listen. He was near hysterics himself. He sped into the hospital emergency room drive and ran around and grabbed George Washington. George was screaming and trying to pull away.

A nurse and Dr. Pooten came out, put George on a stretcher, and strapped him down. About that time, the sheriff pulled in, his siren screaming. Mama, Pappy, and Mammie were right behind him in Mama's car.

The sheriff pulled his gun. Mama and Pappy tackled the stranger and got him on the hospital floor. "If he's hurt my son, I want you to shoot him," said Mama.

"Hurt your son?" said the stranger. "I just saved your son! He was bleeding to death."

Dr. Pooten came out and said that he had given George a sedative, and he was resting comfortably.

"Did you sew him up?" asked the stranger.

"He didn't need sewing up," said Dr. Pooten. "We just washed him up. There wasn't a scratch on that boy. How did he get so bloody, anyway?"

"Hog killing," said Pappy. "George likes to pretend he's a doctor and dissect the innards. He's a real smart boy."

"You all go out in the waiting room and have some coffee," said Dr. Pooten.

We all went to the waiting room and tried to straighten out that big mess. Mama apologized for knocking the stranger down. The stranger apologized for jumping to conclusions and bringing George to the hospital. Pappy apologized to the stranger for hitting him. Mammie wrung her hands and prayed, "Oh thank you Lord for saving our boy."

The sheriff scratched his head in amazement. Dr. Pooten said George was the smartest child he knew, and asked Mama if it would be alright to show George around the hospital. Mama agreed.

"Of course," she said. "I'll bring him by tomorrow. What would be a good time?"

Dr. Pooten was thinking to himself, "I have to ask that woman out. She's the prettiest lady I've ever seen."

The next day, Mama picked George up at the hospital after Dr. Pooten had shown him around. Dr. Pooten got up his nerve to ask Mama out, and they dated for the next fifteen years.

Chapter 6

Preacher Man

Mama said Mammie was quite normal until the Holy Rollers got hold of her and turned her into a religious fanatic.

Mama forbade Mammie to take George and me to Holy Roller church with her. She said it poisoned our minds. Mammie thought it was her duty to lead us down the path of righteousness. When Mama left us over the weekend with Mammie, she would take us to church anyway. She said Mama could like it or lump it.

Mammie would get us up early and tell us to get dressed. George and I would cry and beg not to go. Pappy would make any excuse he could to get out of the house. He didn't want to go, either. Mammie didn't listen. She would slick George's hair down with Brylcream and polish my patent leather shoes with a left over biscuit. Then, she would tell us to sit on the front porch and wait for Aunt Mattie to come by and pick us all up. That, by itself, was traumatic enough.

Aunt Mattie had three very mean children that we had to sit in the back seat with. By the time we got to Holy Roller church, we were crying again because Roger had pulled George's hair and Rose had pinched my legs until they were black and blue.

Religion scared the life out of George and me. I would have nightmares about burning in hell for weeks after Mammie made us go.

The preacher looked like what I thought the devil would look like. He was huge. He had little beady eyes, greasy hair, and a white fleshly face…he just looked nasty! When he got up to preach, his neck veins stood out, and his face turned beet red. He would pound his fist on the podium and scream at the congregation like he was mad at them. Even the songs scared me. "There is power, power, wonder working power, in the precious blood of the lamb," and "There is a fountain filled with blood, flowing from Immanuel's veins." I wondered, "Whose lamb are they talking about, and why is it bleeding into a fountain?"

He mostly liked to preach about everybody going to hell. It seemed to me like the women got the short end of the stick. "Women, the men are the head of the house; you have to cleave unto your man." I guess that means he is the boss and you better do what he says or else. Many times we sat next to families that I knew had taken Preacher Man at his word. The children looked like dogs that had been whupped with a stick. The women had had a good lickin', because they sported a black eye as though it was an automatic ticket to heaven.

Like the Good Book says, "…whoever needs correction shows prudence." I guess those women thought they were being *real* prudent.

The ladies of the congregation weren't too sweet to me, either. They would say, "She's not as p-r-e-t-t-y as Anna is," and I would reply, "I'm very s-m-a-r-t, though."

George and I hated Preacher Man as much as Mammie loved him. The reason being, we thought he was going to throw Mama and Lucy in hell. Lucy was Mama's best friend. They smoked cigarettes, drank wine, wore pants, and cut their hair short. Any of these sins alone, according to Preacher Man, was reason to roast in hell.

Preacher Man did some preaching to George and me, too. "Spare the rod and spoil the child" was one of his favorites. George and I didn't get hit with a rod, and we wondered if maybe Mama was taking us to hell with her because of it.

Women could get a whupping for all kinds of reasons: if they spent too much money, if they got their hair cut (you know, the woman's hair is her crowning glory), if she burned the beans, if she talked back, and if she did anything without permission.

Actually, Mammie's church name was "Jesus Christ Primitive…One Way, God's way…Living World Tabernacle", but Mama and Lucy just called it Holy Roller. Mama and Lucy made all kinds of fun of it when no one was listening.

About half of Pea Ridge went to that church. George and I were afraid to say much when the children in school told us we were going to hell because we didn't truly believe in Holy Roller church. When we asked questions about things we didn't understand, we were told to "trust in the Lord."

We didn't need anybody to tell us how to act. The thought of burning in hell was punishment enough.

One Sunday, when George and I were at Mammie's, Mammie invited the preacher home with us for dinner. She killed a chicken that morning and fried it. I tried not to think about that when I ate chicken; otherwise, that chicken would get bigger and bigger as I chewed it.

City folks don't know how chicken gets to the table, but I do. This morning, that chicken was strutting around the yard just as confident as could be. Mammie fed it some corn, and when it wasn't looking, she caught that chicken around the neck. She slung it around and around by the neck until it drew its last breath. Then, she took the ax and chopped its head off. The headless body flounced around the yard until it was dead. Then, she stuck it in a kettle of boiling water and plucked off all of its feathers. It's enough to make you sick, isn't it?

When we had fried chicken, I would pretend it was chicken that was bought out of the Piggly Wiggly, because Mammie made the best fried chicken and gravy you ever ate. Along with the chicken, Mammie put on a spread. She served fresh string beans, fried corn, fried okra, mashed potatoes, cornbread, and biscuits. For dessert, there was banana pudding and chocolate cake.

I know why that old hell fire preacher was so fat. When we sat down to eat, Mammie served the preacher first. He took out the pulley bone and two pieces of breast. Mattie's children took out both legs and both thighs. Mattie took both wings. That left George and me with the back and neck, and Mama, who had come to pick us up, with nothing.

At home, George and I got the best pieces first.

Mama said, "We don't have enough. George and Ivy don't like the back and the neck"

"Children should be seen and not heard," said Preacher Man. He had his mouth stuffed with chicken breast and mashed potatoes. It was squishing out of the side of his mouth. His poor little wife, who also had no chicken, looked embarrassed.

George whispered to me, "It's not polite to talk with your mouth full."

"Would ya'll like some fried okra?" Mammie asked.

Pappy said, "George and Ivy, I'll get you some banana pudding first."

Mattie said, "You're spoiling George and Ivy. What about my children? They want banana pudding first."

Mattie was Mama's sister, and sometimes she got on Pappy's nerves. Pappy told her to be quiet, and Mama just smiled.

After dinner, the women washed and dried the dishes. The children went out to play kick the can. Pappy said he had to go to Buster's house to help him move his bull. The preacher leaned back in his chair, picked his teeth with a tooth pick, and made a sucking noise, trying to get chicken out of his teeth.

"It's a sin to work on Sunday," Preacher Man said.

Pappy said he didn't care, he was going anyway.

Preacher Man got his Bible and said he was going to Sister Maggie Lee's house to save her soul.

It was rumored that Sister Maggie Lee was a loose woman, but George and I didn't know what that meant.

Sister Maggie Lee wore more Max Factor than anyone I had ever seen. Her blouse was always unbuttoned so you could see her bosom. One time, when she was sitting on the porch with her legs spread apart, George and I were in the yard, and we could see that she wasn't wearing any panties. Maybe Preacher Man was going to tell her if she didn't wear panties, she was going to hell.

Preacher Man was gone a long time.

In the meantime, Mammie said she needed to gather the eggs. She told George and me to get the egg basket. She asked Preacher Man's wife to walk with us to the barn to gather eggs, and she would give his wife some to take home. When we got close to the barn, we heard moaning like someone was hurt real bad. We opened the barn door and you are not going to believe what we saw! Preacher Man's big old white butt was shining. He had his britches down around his ankle, and Sister Maggie Lee had her dress pulled up. They were on a bale of hay, fornicating. George and I had seen Pappy's bull fornicating the cows, so we knew what fornicating was.

George and I took off, just a-flying back toward the house. Pappy was back from Buster's house by then, and he and Mama were coming out the door. We started screaming, "Preacher Man's fornicating Sister Maggie Lee! Preacher Man's fornicating Sister Maggie Lee!"

"What are you talking about?" asked Pappy

"We saw Preacher Man fornicating Sister Maggie Lee," I said.

Mama said, "Ivy, tell me exactly what you saw."

"I saw Preacher Man with his britches around his ankles on top of Sister Maggie Lee," I said.

George said, "I saw Preacher Man's big old white butt."

Mammie came to the house. She was as white as a sheet. Preacher Man's wife was crying. The preacher wasn't far behind, swinging his belt in the air. He raised his belt to us. "Lying young'uns! Lying young'uns! I'm going to whup the devil out of them." Pappy grabbed Preacher Man's wrist and Mama balled up her fist and hit him square in the nose. Blood started squirting everywhere. She had broken it!

"You son of a bitch! If you ever look at my children again, I'm going to kill you," said Mama.

Preacher Man's wife said, "He did the same thing at our last church. That's why we had to move."

Pappy said, "You either quit preaching or I'm going to tell everybody what you did."

Preacher Man was gone by the next Sunday. The church members started going other places to worship, and the church finally closed its doors forever. George and I were sure glad of that.

We heard from Preacher Man one more time before he left. He, for sure, wished he hadn't tangled with Mama and Lucy. After teaching school for all those years, Mama and Lucy had some friends in low places as well as in high places.

Preacher Man moved, but before he did, he started an ugly rumor that Mama and Lucy were atheist. Lucy and Mama could handle a challenge. They did it daily while running a school. Lucy was the principal, and Mama was a teacher, but she was also Lucy's best friend.

Lucy and Mama talked it over and they decided they wouldn't let Preacher get by with spreading that rumor.

A few years back, they had helped a boy named Hoss stay out of jail. They went to court and told the judge that Hoss was a good boy, although a bit misguided, so the judge just let him go with a warning.

Mama and Lucy called Hoss and told him the situation. Hoss loved Mama and Lucy, and he would do anything for them. Well, Hoss got Preacher Man out behind a barn and beat the stew out of him. Then he stole Preacher Man's clothes. Preacher Man had to walk back into town buck naked and bleeding.

"Hoss, we said scare him, not kill him" said Lucy.

Well, you'uns is the most Christian people I've ever knowed," said Hoss. "It ain't right, him doing that to ya'll."

The sheriff was Lucy's cousin, and he didn't do a thing to Mama and Lucy, or even Hoss.

Old Preacher Man tucked his tail between his legs and left town, never to be seen or heard from again.

Chapter 7

▼

The Modernization of Mammie

After that unfortunate incident with Preacher Man, Mammie just wasn't the same. Mama took this as an omen to start getting Mammie back to her old self, like she was before she became a Holy Roller. George and I were all for that.

I don't know how Mama was the fruit of Mammie's loins. They were nothing alike. Mama was a beautiful, fiery, free-thinking woman. Mammie was old fashioned, strict with George and me, and a tight wad.

Mama would let George and me do anything as long as we didn't hurt ourselves or someone else.

One time, George wore a nylon stocking on his head for a week. He was trying to make his frizzy hair lay down. Someone asked Mama why she let him do that, and she said she was letting him express himself. The truth was, she hadn't really noticed.

I know Mama loved Mammie, but they couldn't get along for two seconds. Mammie tried to boss Mama around. Mama had a strong will and wouldn't listen.

Mama and I had lived with Mammie and Pappy after my Daddy was killed in the war. While Mama finished college, Mammie kept me. Mama knew she had to get a job as a teacher so she could raise me.

Mama's and Mammie's conversation went something like this:

"You need to visit me more often," Mammie would say.

"I would if you weren't so bossy," Mama would say.

"I'm afraid you're going to hell for smoking and drinking wine," Mammie would reply.

"Mind your own business, and you won't have to mind mine," Mama would argue back.

The Good Book says, "Honor thy father and thy mother". But you get the idea…they just could not get along.

Mama usually got her way because she was so stubborn. So, when she decided she was going to make some changes in Mammie's life, she meant business. Mama loved a challenge.

The first thing she did was to change Mammie's name. This was the easy part. She wouldn't let George or me call her Mammie any more. She said that calling her that sounded ignorant.

Mammie said that Mattie's children called her "Mammie" and Mama said that just proved it was ignorant.

Mama said that we could call Mammie "Mama June" and we could call Pappy "Papa Jake". Mammie wouldn't answer us for the longest time when we called her "Mama June", but finally she accepted that that was the way it was going to be.

The next thing Mama tackled was the way Mama June looked. Mama June made her own clothes. Some of them were made out of flour sacks. Mama, on the other hand, was always stylishly dressed. She wore Bobbie Brooks pants, every time she could. Mama June used the same pattern over and over to save money, so most of her dresses looked alike…flowered and with a white collar.

Mama got her hair fixed at the beauty shop every Saturday. Mama June wore her long gray hair in two plats pulled to the top of her head.

Mama started to work on Mama June to get her to change her ways. Mama June moped around for about two weeks while Mama worked on her. Mama said she needed to snap out of it. Mama said she needed to get her hair cut and get her some pants. Mama June said that Papa Jake wore the pants in the family. Mama said Mama June needed to wear some makeup, and Mama June said that might be a sin.

Mama always drove a nice car. Mama June couldn't drive. She said that driving was the man's job. Mama June's age was 60, but she looked and acted over 70.

It took months, but Mama got what she wanted.

We picked Mama June up one Saturday morning and drove to Nashville. Mama pulled up in front of the best beauty shop in the state of Tennessee. She told the owner, "I want a complete make-over for my mother."

Mama June started praying, and then she took a nerve pill.

The hair stylist cut, styled, and colored Mama June's hair. When she was done with that, the make-up artist made up Mama June's face.

Mama June couldn't believe it when they were finished and she looked in the mirror. She was the prettiest thing you ever laid eyes on. Her hair was blond, not gray; and it was short and curly. Her face looked twenty years younger. Mama June was never the same after that.

Mama took her to Harvey's and bought her seven new outfits, including pants.

When we got back to the farm, Mama June announced that she was going to learn how to drive. Mama and Papa Jake both said they would teach her.

Papa Jake was delighted with the way Mama June looked. I caught him patting her on the butt more than one time.

Mama June had a new lease on life, and she wasn't about to let anybody change that.

Aunt Mattie came by one day and said she wanted some biscuits. Mama June made the best biscuits in the county, but she said, "Make them yourself. I've got a club meeting today."

Once, Mama said, "I'm bringing George and Ivy by today."

Mama June said, "They can stay with Jake. I'm going shopping with Gladys in Nashville. Then we're going to eat out. I won't be home until about 10 o'clock tonight.

Papa Jake asked, "When are we going to kill hogs this year?"

Mama June said, "You can kill all the hogs you want to. *I'm* going to register for college. I've always wanted a college degree.

Papa Jake liked Mama June that way. It was the strangest thing I've ever witnessed in my life. Papa Jake liked her so much that he went out and bought her a brand new red Cadillac convertible for Christmas. He didn't even complain when she served him bologna and cold pork and beans five nights in a row, because of her shopping trips and her club meetings.

Mama June said that she had seen the light. She didn't cook; she didn't clean; she didn't sew; she didn't garden. She and Papa Jake went dancing. Eventually, they sold the farm and moved to town.

"This is disgraceful," said Mama June's old friends from the church.

"She's had a nervous breakdown," said Aunt Mattie. "It's all Anna's fault. You know how she's always messing everything up for everybody. Anna thinks she's better than anybody else because she went to college." Aunt Mattie was in a rage.

"Now, Mattie, Anna worked very hard to send herself to college," said Mama June.

"We would have sent you and paid for it," said Papa Jake, "but you took your college money and spent it on a trip to China."

"You wanted to be a missionary," said Mama June.

"And you were back in two weeks," said Papa Jake.

"Mammie, you always loved Anna the best," said Mattie.

Mama June said, "Please don't ever call me "Mammie" again. I'm not a "Mammie". Call me "June". Call me "Mama June". Call me "Jake's Wife". But never, ever, call me "Mammie" again.

Aunt Mattie stormed out of the house and slammed the door.

We sure liked Mama June a lot better after she got modernized. Mama June needed to do a little payback and help Mama with her cooking…but she never got around to it.

Chapter 8

A Cool Sip of Water

I had the idea to sell spring water long before it became popular to buy it in bottles.

After Mama June became modernized, she didn't pay any more attention to George and me than Mama did. We could get by with anything. When George and I decided to become business partners, Mama June was in Nashville. She didn't know anything about our plans.

Mama June and Papa Jake had a fresh water spring on their farm. It had the best cold water you ever tasted. Before the Tennessee Valley Authority made Center Hill Dam, people in our county had no electricity. Springs served as their refrigerator. Mama June and Papa Jake would put their milk and butter in the spring in the morning, and by supper time, it would be good and cold.

Road workers usually stopped at the spring to get a fresh drink of water and to rest in the shade, or eat their salted fatback and cold biscuit for lunch.

George and I were enterprising children, so we planned and planned how to make money. We knew the peddler came every Tuesday, and we wanted to buy candy from him. We could stock up and hide it, and nobody would ever know. Mama didn't allow us to eat candy…she said it would rot out our teeth. My favorite food was candy.

I got the idea that the road workers would have to pay George and me for their water. We gathered up some of Mama June's fruit jars…she would never miss them. After her modernization, she wasn't going to make any more preserves.

We took the jars down to the spring and filled them up with water. We got some two-by-four boards and rocks and built a barricade across the path to the spring. Then we made a sign: "Fresh Cool Water 5¢ A Jar".

We were in business…bottled water!

We heard the road workers coming down the road.

"I'm so dry I could fart dust," said Earl, as they turned down the path. They came face to face with George and me.

"Water…five cents," I said.

"Does Jake know you're doing this?" Earl asked.

"Yep, it was his idea," I lied.

"Let me go over to the house and ask your Pappy about this," said Hank.

"Just give her a nickel," said Earl. "I'm too hot to argue about it."

They bought their water, and so did the other road workers. George and I were getting richer…5¢, 10¢, 15¢, 20¢. Together, we had 40¢.

The road workers sat down by the spring. One of the workers fanned his face with his gray felt hat and another wiped sweat from his forehead with a red bandana. This wasn't such a bad deal for them…they didn't have to take turns drinking from the dipper.

The peddler came by that afternoon, and we bought four candy bars each. Candy was a nickel a bar. I bought my favorite…Baby Ruth. I always ate the outside layer of nuts and chocolate first, like an ear of corn. Then, I ate the maple fudge in the middle.

I had never in my life eaten all the candy I wanted.

Mr. Thurman was the peddler. "Where'd ya'll get all that money?" he asked us.

"Papa Jake gave it to us," we lied.

"Does Anna know ya'll are buying all this candy?"

He is so nosy, I thought. "Yep", I replied.

"She gives us candy all the time," lied George.

After the peddler left, George and I went across the road and sat down on a rock. We each unwrapped a candy bar. It was so good; I stuffed half of mine in my mouth at once.

The plan had been to eat just one candy bar each, and hide the rest for later. Sometimes, though, the best plans just don't work out.

"Let's eat another one," I said. George already had half of his second bar in his mouth.

We each ate four candy bars.

"I don't feel so good," I moaned.

I ran behind a tree and threw up, and this made George throw up.

We washed our hands and faces and lay in the grass until we felt better.

Mama June came home and we went back to the house.

"I've got a surprise for you," she said, as she pulled out a pound of fudge.

"Mama won't let us eat candy," we both groaned at the same time.

Chapter 9

Goin' Fishin'

George was a big old prissy butt, a sissy, but he was my best friend, and I didn't like for the jerks in our class to call him prissy or sissy. I called them ugly names back, I told on them, I did everything I could think of, but to no avail. Nothing worked, so I decided George would just have to act more like the other boys in our class. I don't know why I wanted that, though…I hated the boys in our class.

I talked this over with Big Daddy…he told me the same thing that Mama did. "Just give him a little time," he said. "He won't always be a sissy."

"But Big Daddy, they are mean to him and I hate it. Can't we do something? Can't you teach him something manly?"

"Well, how about hunting?"

I was horrified. George would never kill a living animal, except at hog killing time.

"Well, how about football?"

"Big Daddy, honestly…you're joking. They would *kill* him."

"I guess you're right. The only other thing I can think of would be fishing."

"Perfect." Why didn't we think of that sooner?"

Big Daddy went out and bought George a brand new fishing pole, floats, hooks, a tackle box, and bait. They put it all in Big Daddy's truck and went to the river that ran through Big Daddy's farm.

George was complaining the whole time. He had to get up too early. He didn't want to get dirty. He sure was not going to touch a worm. (This was from a boy who could dissect an entire hog.)

They got to the river, and Big Daddy put the worm on George's hook. George threw out his line and caught it on a weed. He jerked it really hard and the line came flying back. The hook caught George in the nostril!

It took Big Daddy a minute to realize what had happened. There stood poor George with a fish hook in his nose. His fishing career ended after five minutes.

Big Daddy loaded everything up and got George in the truck. He tried once to get the fish hook out of George's nose, but George started crying and screaming, so Big Daddy drove him straight to the hospital. Dr. Pooten met them at the hospital door. He took George back to the operating room and gave him a shot to calm him down. Then he got some wire cutters from Big Daddy, cut the hook, and removed it in two pieces.

I think this is the only time that Dr. Pooten ever got really mad at me. That night, when he came to see us, he called me into the kitchen. "Alice Ivy, you have got to leave George alone. You are being meaner to him than the boys in your class."

I started to cry, "I didn't mean for George to get hurt.

"I know, but everybody is different. I don't like to get dirty, I don't like to chew tobacco, I don't like to run and sweat, I don't like to be beat up on the football field, but I don't consider myself a sissy. George is smart. He'll grow up just fine. So, just quit trying to help him, before you cause some real damage. So far you have made him smoke rabbit tobacco, which made him deathly ill, and now you're involving him with your Big Daddy and fishing. Alice Ivy, you are dangerous!"

I knew I shouldn't have said it, but it just popped out of my mouth, anyway. "But Dr. Pooten, George is mine. Mama got him for me when I was in the 4th grade. (I was in the sixth grade then).

"Alice Ivy, I'm ashamed of you!" exclaimed Dr. Pooten. "Nobody belongs to anybody else. We are all individuals with a will of our own. Now, I think you had better go and apologize to George, and promise him you'll be nice to him from now on."

I did. I apologized and promised George that I would quit tormenting him.

George was very nice about the whole thing.

Chapter 10

Big'un and Big'un's Brother

Big'un and Big'un's brother were twins, and they were really fat. They had a habit of letting their mouths hang open, and sometimes a little dribble of slobber would run down their chins. They were not retarded, but they were a little slow. It took too much energy for them to hold their mouths shut.

Their mama dressed them just alike, usually in blue jeans with the cuffs rolled up, a white T-shirt, and a belt pulled really tight at the waist. That made them look like a pillow tied in the middle. They usually wore white socks and red high top tennis shoes.

Their mama looked just like them, with longer hair. She talked really loud, and she was an expert on everything…especially education. Our mama would hide in the teacher's workroom closet every time she heard their mama coming. Their mama was always trying to tell our mama how to teach. There was no doubt, she loved her boys.

Mrs. Peeler, their mama, drove an old Woody station wagon. Her job was selling Watkins Products. Big'un and Big'un's brother always had a faint smell of Watkins liniment about them, and they were always hungry.

Most of the children in our class ate school lunch, and about half of them got free lunch, including Big'un and Big'un's brother.

George and I always brought our lunch to school. This is one of the reasons why we got picked on. George and I didn't like the school lunch, and neither did Mama.

Our lunch was always good: a bologna sausage sandwich with mustard and cheese, crackers, sometimes a banana, and a dessert. George made the best desserts…homemade tea cakes, chocolate cake, and brownies were his specialty.

The children who sat with us at the lunch table would beg for our food. We were nice children, so we would give them just a little bite. We felt bad for them because the school lunch left a lot to be desired. They would have canned meat (probably horse), canned green beans (cold and no seasoning), runny mashed potatoes, light bread, and canned cling peaches. We felt rich and fortunate not to have to eat the school lunch.

Big'un and Big'un's brother had about enough of watching us eat our home-made lunch while they had to eat the school lunch. Some of the other country children, whose parents wouldn't let them eat free lunch, brought their lunch, too. Their lunch looked worse than the school lunch…cold meat and a biscuit, a cold baked sweet potato, corn bread, and maybe a wormy apple.

Big'un and Big'un's brother loved food more than anything. They were not of the highest moral fiber, so one day they stole our lunch, went out behind the school and gobbled it down. Then, they came in the lunch room and ate their free school lunch.

George and I had to eat the school lunch that day, or at least, we ate the cling peaches. We got really hungry in the afternoon.

Big'un and Big'un's brother didn't get caught, so they stole our lunch every day for two weeks in a row. George and I got really tired of it, too. Of course, they lied about it. They would say, "You saw us eat the school lunch."

George and I had a couple of choices to make: either teach Big'un and Big'un's brother a lesson, or keep providing them with lunch every day. We decided they needed the lesson, bad. After all, everybody knows stealing is a sin, and they could wind up in hell, we reasoned.

It took us forever, but we saved up our money until we had $2.00. We would walk to the drug store and buy a box of Ex-Lax every day until we had spent our $2.00.

We had to do this secretly. Mama knew nothing about it, except she knew we had our lunch stolen several times. She told us to try and solve the problem ourselves, and if we couldn't, she would tell Lucy to take care of it.

One day, Mama went to the drug store to buy some lipstick. The pharmacist asked Mama if she was constipated. This embarrassed her, so she shouted, "Abel

Jones! That is none of your business, and furthermore, that is a disgusting thing to ask a lady!"

Poor Abel had a crush on Mama and the last thing he wanted to do was to make her mad.

"I didn't mean any harm, Anna…I was just going to recommend some medicine," said Abel.

"Shut up! Shut up!" shouted Mama, and she stormed out of the drug store, her face as red as a beet.

We decided that George would bake some "special" brownies for us to put in our lunches. George had to bake the brownies before Mama got home from faculty meeting. George followed the recipe exactly: *3 eggs, 2 cups sugar, 1 cup flour, 1 c. butter, 3 squares chocolate* and this is where he substituted *3 boxes Ex-Lax.*

When the brownies were done, George made Ex-Lax icing. We took the tiniest little bite. They were not as good as George's regular brownies, but they were alright. Besides, Big'un and Big'un's brother gobbled everything down without taking much time to savor the taste.

We wrapped the brownies in wax paper and put them in George's closet. The next morning, we put the whole batch in our lunch bags. Sure enough, when the lunch bell rang, we couldn't find our lunches!

I asked to be excused and went to see what Big'un and Big'un's brother were doing. As we expected, they went running out behind the school. They were laughing as they pulled our lunches out from under their shirts. They gobbled down four brownies each. They just shoved the whole brownie in their mouths, chewed twice, and swallowed.

On the first brownie Big'un said, "These good!"

By the fourth brownie Big'un's brother said, "These ain't as good as them teacakes, though."

They ate some more, and then shoved the bags in a hole under the school house.

George and I went in the lunch room and ate our cling peaches. School lunch didn't taste so bad that day.

After lunch, everybody went back to the room, and Mama started class.

About 1:00, Big'un said, "Miss Anna, I got to go!" and ran out of the room. Big'un's brother was right behind him.

In a few minutes they came back. They no sooner sat down, than Big'un's brother said, "May I be excused?" and they left running again. This went on for an hour.

They were green around the mouth.

George whispered to me, "I think we might have put too much Ex-Lax in!"

The whole class gasped when Big'un started to heave. Nothing came up…just dry heaves.

Mama took Big'un and his brother to the office.

"I think you need to call Dr. Pooten for these boys! Something's wrong with them," Mama said to Lucy.

Lucy got both boys in the car and rushed them to the hospital.

Dr. Pooten examined them and then he called their mama.

When Mrs. Peeler got there, she rushed in and said, "I told ya'll not to eat too many of them green apples, didn't I?"

"Yes'm," replied Big'un.

Dr. Pooten was puzzled. "How many green apples did you eat?"

He kept them in the hospital over night. He thought they might have been poisoned. He asked their mama, "Do you have rats in your house? Have you been using D-Con?"

"I didn't poison my boys," Mrs. Peeler said. "It's them green apples!"

Dr. Pooten asked, "What did you eat last?"

"We et school lunch…meat, beans, 'taters, and light bread," said Big'un's brother.

Dr. Pooten got on the phone and called Lucy. "Are any of the other children sick?"

"Not that I know of," said Lucy.

Big'un and Big'un's brother couldn't tell Dr. Pooten or their mama about eating our lunches because they had stolen them and they knew they would get in big trouble for stealing.

I don't think they figured out it was the brownies that put them in the hospital, because if they had, they would have surely beaten us up.

Big'un and his brother had to stay out of school for a week. When they came back they had lost ten pounds apiece, and they still looked peaked.

Their mama came to the school and accused the lunch room ladies of poisoning her boys.

George and I were scared to death. We really didn't mean to nearly kill Big'un and Big'un's brother. We were just tired of eating cling peaches.

Big'un and his brother would never eat chocolate again. When they even looked at chocolate, they would turn white around the mouth and gag.

George and I decided we had really done them a big favor because after they gave up chocolate they started to "fall off" (lose weight). We might have even saved their souls too, because they stopped stealing.

George and I could keep a secret. We never told on ourselves and Mama never found out about our Ex-Lax brownies.

Dr. Pooten never could figure out what was wrong with the twins, either. George and I were lucky, indeed!

Chapter 11

Cora Lee Poor Thing

Miss Cora Lee Jernigan was always sick or nervous or constipated. She was Mama June's neighbor. When George and I would visit Mama June, Miss Cora Lee would call and say she had something for us to do, and she would give us a nickel.

George and I didn't like Cora Lee at all. She was always telling us she was constipated or telling us about some other ailment she had. She didn't smell good, and her house was downright nasty. She wouldn't allow us to laugh or run in the house or talk loud. She said we made her nervous.

We would tell Mama June we didn't want to go, but Mama June would lay a guilt trip on us.

"Cora Lee, poor thing, she needs your help."

"Cora Lee, poor thing, she is so sick."

"Cora Lee, poor thing, can't do a thing."

George and I started calling her "Cora Lee Poor Thing."

Well, Cora Lee Poor Thing called Mama June and said she needed George and me to come and churn butter for her. Mama June made us go. We walked as slowly as we could, dreading being around Cora Lee Poor Thing. Cora Lee Poor Thing was waiting for us on the porch.

After she put us to work churning, Cora Lee Poor Thing went to bed with a sick headache. We churned and churned and churned…and nothing happened!

Mama always bought margarine for George to cook with. It was the kind that was white, with a package of yellow dye that you worked into it to make it yellow.

George got an idea. He said, "Ivy, I'm tired of this churning, and it's almost supper time. Let's get some lard from the lard stand, and some yellow food coloring, and make margarine. We can put it in the milk and nobody will know the difference."

We slipped into the kitchen and George got six big handfuls of lard out of the lard stand. I found the food coloring.

We worked and worked until the lard was yellow. We took the lard to the porch and put it in the churn full of milk. Then we told Cora Lee Poor Thing that we had to go back to Mama June's house for supper.

Cora Lee Poor Thing asked, "Why don't you just eat here with me?"

I *knew* we were not going to do that. Flies were everywhere. A sore-eyed cat lay right in the middle of the table. We saw some old cold biscuits and some fat back sitting on the table. That's probably what she was going to feed us!

Cora Lee Poor Thing came out and looked at the butter-lard. She said it looked good and rich, and it sure made a lot! She gave us our nickel and went back to bed.

George and I went back to Mama June's and had a bologna sausage sandwich and some cold pork and beans for supper.

Mama June asked us if we got our money. We said that we did, but we thought she would give each of us a nickel. She gave us only one nickel to share.

The next day was Sunday, and Cora Lee Poor Thing was going to church and "dinner on the ground" at the Sugar Tree Baptist Church. Mama June occasionally went to the Baptist church, since she was no longer a Holy Roller.

Mama June took us to church that day. We were horrified when we saw what Cora Lee Poor Thing had brought to eat. It was corn bread and our butter-lard!

People in those days were polite. They knew that Cora Lee's kitchen was nasty, but they took some corn bread and butter anyway.

Not George and me! We said we couldn't eat a bite! There was some really good food there, and we were hungry, but we knew we weren't going to chance having to eat that corn bread and butter.

People started eating that corn bread and butter and as soon as they tasted it, they spit it out. Some of the ladies tried to spit it in a napkin without being noticed, but the men didn't mind being noticed. They just spit out big mouthfuls on the ground.

"Cora Lee, what on earth is wrong with this butter?" one of the ladies asked. "What's them cows been eating—ragweed?"

Cora Lee Poor Thing started crying. "I don't know why you good, Christian people have to be so mean to me. You know when I get nervous, I get a sick headache!'

Mama June said, "Jake, get the young'uns in the truck. We've got to go home."

We knew we were in some serious trouble.

Papa Jake said, "Let me get them a piece of that corn bread and some of that butter to eat in the back of the truck as we drive home."

Mama June knew we had something to do with that butter. She made us eat a whole piece of that corn bread with lard-butter on it. That was our punishment.

Cora Lee Poor Thing never did ask us to churn for her again, but she never knew exactly what we did to that butter. She never asked Mama June for us to work for her, either.

Mama June was shed of Cora Lee's poor, pitiful self, so I guess everything worked out pretty good…except that George and I were as sick as a dog for a day or two.

Chapter 12

Bucky

Aunt Martha lived down the road from Bucky. George and I were out in her yard, playing with hedge apples, when we heard the most God-awful noise. We thought it was a sick animal or something. We went to investigate and found it was coming from Bucky's house. We had never seen Bucky, but we had heard a rumor that a crazy person lived there.

We walked over to his house and peeked in the windows. We saw Bucky, and he was terrible looking. His head was big, his face was flat, and his eyes were slanted. He was throwing a fit, or something. We found out later that when he threw a fit, his parents would lock him in his room until he calmed down.

George motioned for him to come to the window. Bucky jumped up and down and made a noise.

"Let's get him out of there," I said.

We opened the window. George crawled in the window and I followed. We eased over to Bucky and took his hand. We led him over to the window and helped him get out. I guess his folks didn't take him out much, because as soon as he got out of the window, he took off running.

George and I caught up with him. He was carrying a big wooden spoon, and he just about beat the stew out of George and me before we got him calmed down and back in his room. That was the first time we met Bucky.

The next week, when Mama and Lucy went to Nashville with Rachel, we visited Aunt Martha again. We slipped over to Bucky's house. This time we were prepared…we thought.

George had gone to the library and checked out *Cinderella, Goldilocks and the Three Bears*, and *The Three Little Pigs*. We were going to read to Bucky.

Bucky was about twenty years old, and he was huge. We had no idea what we were dealing with.

George helped Bucky get out through the window. We went out of sight, down in the woods, and found a nice place to sit and read.

George started reading and Bucky loved it. I guess nobody had ever read to him before. As George read, Bucky repeated everything George said.

"Cin-der-rella, rella, rella," said Bucky, and every time he said "rella" he bopped George on the head with his big wooden spoon.

George read for a while, but finally, he couldn't take it any more. We started trying to get Bucky back in his room. Bucky threw a big old fit, but somehow we got him through the window and in his room without getting caught.

The third time we slipped over to Bucky's house, we weren't so lucky.

George was reading *Cinderella* to Bucky, again. Bucky got so excited about *Cinderella* that he started to wet his pants. He had a big wet spot right in front of his pants. I told George that he needed to show Bucky how to pee.

George objected, but I said that Bucky was just going to keep on wetting his pants until he learned how. I said, "I won't look. Just go behind that tree."

George showed him how, and Bucky thought it was the grandest thing. He started watering all the trees and bushes. George made him stop, but he had to take a beating with the wooden spoon.

I told George that we'd better get Bucky back in his room before we got caught. Things were progressing nicely, until a car came down the road. It was Clarence Biggs and his wife, and Bucky started chasing the car. Mr. Biggs stopped the car, and he and his wife got out.

"Does Cecil know you got this boy out?" he asked.

"Sure," I said. "We're teaching him. George just taught him how to pee."

About that time, Bucky gave Mr. Biggs a bop on the head with his spoon.

"Ya'll get that boy home," Mr. Biggs said. Mr. Biggs and his wife got back in the car, and they drove up Cecil's driveway. Mr. Biggs walked up to the front door and started knocking. We knew we were in bad trouble.

Bucky was hitting Mr. Biggs' car with his spoon when Cecil came out of the front door. Cecil had a shotgun in his hand.

"I'm going to have you young'uns arrested for kidnapping," he said to George and me.

"Now, pipe down, Cecil," Mr. Biggs said. "I don't think they meant no harm."

Cecil ranted and raved some more. I had to think fast.

"George taught him how to pee," I said.

"That boy can't pee by himself," Cecil said.

"Yes he can," George said. "Show him, Bucky."

Bucky showed them, right there in the front yard.

"He can talk, too," I said. "Say 'Cinderella.'"

"Cin-der-rella, rella, rella," Bucky yelled, as he bopped George on the head with the spoon.

Cecil got Bucky back in his room, and he took George and me back to Aunt Martha's. He told her what had happened.

Aunt Martha looked mad, but I could tell that she really wasn't. George and I had made a life long friend.

When Mama picked us up, we told her the whole story.

Mama loved a cause. When we got home, she told George to make one of his famous chocolate cakes.

The next day, she put us in the car. We drove over to Bucky's house, got out, and knocked on the door with that delicious chocolate cake. Cecil had gone to town, but Mrs. Bone came to the door. When she opened the door, she looked dragged out and pitiful.

Mama apologized for George and me kidnapping Bucky. Then she said, "Why don't we have some cake?"

Mama said that George and I really liked Bucky, and asked if we could come back to play with him when we came to visit Aunt Martha.

That scared Mrs. Bone to death. She said that she and Cecil were afraid Bucky would hurt us. We said that we weren't afraid of Bucky at all…but the spoon was kind of painful on George's head.

Chapter 13

Bucky's First Christmas

Poor Bucky had been locked in his room for the past 20 years. His parents weren't particularly cruel…they were just ignorant and uneducated.

Mama enlightened them as best she could. She told them that Bucky could learn and work, and be helpful on the farm. Cecil told Mama she was crazy and she ought to mind her own business.

I was so proud of Mrs. Bone. She said, "Why don't we give Bucky a chance?" He was her son, too, and she said it couldn't hurt.

George and I worked diligently in teaching Bucky to clean his room, pick up sticks in the yard…George even showed him how to scramble eggs.

It took the longest time, but eventually we taught him to read and write.

We did the best we could in teaching him to eat vegetables and fruit. He wouldn't touch a bite until George and I ate them first. If he didn't like what we brought him to eat, he would spit it all over the table.

We knew we had to do something because we wanted to bring Bucky to Dr. Pooten's for Christmas, and Tibby wouldn't be very happy that peas were spit all over her table.

We taught Bucky to say "no thank you" instead of spitting. We taught him to eat a few things by rewarding him with bananas. Bucky loved bananas.

Twenty years of neglect wasn't easy to overcome, but George and I were determined to socialize Bucky, and eventually we did.

Bucky didn't know what Christmas was. George and I threw a fit when we found that out. We asked Cecil what he was getting Bucky for Christmas, and Cecil said he "didn't have no money for that kind of foolishness."

We begged Mama and Dr. Pooten to let us bring Bucky to Dr. Pooten's for Christmas. They both said no, they didn't think that was a good idea.

Then, that evening we overheard Mama tell Dr. Pooten that Cecil wouldn't possibly let Bucky out of the house. So, the next day, they said we could bring him.

We had a few weeks before Christmas, so we started working on Cecil and his wife. Eventually, Cecil said we could come and get Bucky to spend Christmas day at Dr. Pooten's house.

Every Christmas, before we met Bucky, George and I would rack up on gifts. We would ask for everything in the Sears and Roebuck catalog, and we got most of them. But this Christmas was different. We debated back and forth…we want everything in the catalog…we want to give Bucky something; we want everything…we want to give Bucky things he needs. We didn't think his parents would give him anything.

Finally, goodness won. We told Mama that all we wanted was money, and a lot of it.

Since we couldn't drive legally because we weren't old enough, we had to tell Mama our plan. She started hugging us.

"My precious children, you are such wonderful human beings," said Mama. She didn't know how we had struggled with goodness. We really *loved* getting those gifts!

We told her that we were going to give Bucky the best Christmas he had ever had. This was true because he had never had Christmas.

She drove us to Nashville and we shopped all day. The first things we bought were pencils, paper, crayons, books, puzzles, and a ball.

Poor Bucky wore pajamas and house shoes all of the time, so we wanted to buy him some decent clothes. This required us to measure him from head to toe. He wasn't too crazy about that, but we told him if he was good, we'd give him a banana, so he cooperated.

We went shopping for clothes. We bought him some blue jeans, shirts, socks, and a belt. George bought him some underwear. He said Bucky's underwear was homemade, and he had to have good underwear in case he was in a wreck and had to go to the hospital.

We bought him a razor, shaving cream, a comb, and some Vitalis Hair Lotion. Then we ran out of money.

We knew we were getting nothing for Christmas, but that was just fine with us. We had the best feeling…to do something good for the less fortunate.

Chapter 14

Cecil

Cecil and Lurlene had married late in life. Cecil was the happiest man on earth when Lurlene told him they were going to have a baby.

When the baby turned out to be a boy, Cecil was in heaven. But things didn't turn out right.

At first, Cecil carried Bucky around all of the time and showed him off to all of his friends. As Bucky grew, they knew something was wrong. He just wasn't developing properly, and Cecil and Lurlene were heart broken.

Bucky didn't walk or talk or sit up until he was four years old. Lurlene tried really hard, but eventually, Cecil and Lurlene gave up and accepted the fact that Bucky would never be like other children.

When the Green children (that was George and me) kidnapped Bucky, Cecil was fighting mad.

George and I involved Mama in our mission to rescue Bucky. Eventually, Cecil gave up trying to get shed of us. He didn't like us, but he tolerated us.

When Christmas came, we learned that he liked us better than we thought.

Christmas day finally came. Mama, George, and I went to pick up Bucky at about 8:00 in the morning. When we got there, Bucky came running out of the house in brand new clothes. He had a new shirt, overalls, new shoes, and a coat. He was grinning from ear to ear.

"Look what Daddy got me," he said.

Lurlene came out the door carrying two Christmas packages. "Cecil got ya'll a present," she said, as she handed the gifts to Mama.

Bucky wasn't very used to riding in a car. We had to make him stop rolling the windows up and down.

When we got to Dr. Pooten's house, Tibby had a big Christmas breakfast cooking. Tibby was a wonderful cook. She didn't cook stuff like ordinary people ate. We had eggs Benedict, fresh fruit, crepes, and beignets.

Tibby was Cajun. We knew that Bucky had better be on his best behavior, or suffer the wrath of Tibby. We had our bananas ready.

"What's this stuff?" asked Bucky.

"Just taste it," said George. "It's eggs Benedict, crepes, and beignets. It's really good."

Bucky took a bite. "I like this stuff," he said.

He ate so much that we had to tell him he couldn't have any more.

We had done such a good job with Bucky's manners. We were proud of ourselves.

However, when it was time to open gifts, we had a tiny problem.

Chapter 15

Bucky, Put Dr. Pooten Down!

When Bucky opened the huge box from Dr. Pooten and saw the bicycle inside, he was so excited that he hugged Dr. Pooten. Then, he picked Dr. Pooten up and swung him around.

"Bucky! You put Dr. Pooten down this minute," George and I yelled at the same time.

Dr. Pooten had a look of pure terror on his face.

"Dr. Pooten doesn't like to be picked up," I said.

"But I love him," said Bucky, "and he gave me a new bicycle!"

"We know," I said, "but we love him too, and we don't want you to hurt him."

Bucky dropped Dr. Pooten like a hot potato. "I would never hurt Dr. Boot," said Bucky, who couldn't talk plain, yet.

Dr. Pooten got up off the floor and straightened his tie. "I think you should teach Bucky how to shake hands."

"That's a real good idea," George and I said at the same time.

When it was time for us to open our present from Bucky, he was so excited.

"Open mine! Open mine!" he said. "I picked it out myself. Daddy took me to town in the truck. He got mad at me for rolling the windows up and down, but he let me buy you a present, anyway."

I opened mine, and it was a beautiful doll with eyes that opened and closed, long hair, and a lace dress. Now, I was way too old for dolls, but I still have that doll today. I love her.

George opened his present. It was a fishing pole. Well, you remember George's experience with fishing!

"I guess I'll just have to give fishing another try," he said.

That turned out to be the best Christmas we ever had.

Chapter 16

Aunt Udy's Corset

One of Aunt Mattie's stupid children couldn't talk plain, so she called Aunt Judy, "Aunt Udy", and it stuck. Everybody started calling her "Aunt Udy"…everybody, that is, except George and me. Mama wouldn't let us.

Aunt Udy complained to Mama that she was fat and couldn't find any cute clothes to wear. Well, Mama was in hog heaven! Mama could nose into other people's business, which was her favorite thing to do.

"Order yourself a corset from the Sears and Roebuck catalog," said Mama. Maybe she *should* have told Aunt Udy, "Quit eating pie."

We got the Sears and Roebuck catalog down off the shelf and they started shopping. Mama said the one that laced down the front might be the best.

Aunt Udy said, "That one costs $5.95. That's a lot of money. Maybe a girdle would be just as good."

Mama, who had a beautiful figure, said, "No, I believe a corset would hold you in better."

Mama filled out the order blank before Aunt Udy had time to think.

"I'll drop this in the mail, Aunt Judy." Mama refused to call Aunt Judy, "Aunt Udy."

Aunt Udy went to the mail box every day for two weeks. Finally, the corset came. Aunt Udy called us and we drove over to her house. We opened the package.

I had never seen a corset before, but it looked awful, like something you would use to torture somebody you hated.

Mama and Aunt Udy went in the bedroom. Aunt Udy took off her dress and Mama started lacing her in the corset, but Mama couldn't get it laced tight enough.

George and I were in the living room playing Chinese checkers. "George, Ivy," she called, "come in here. I need your help."

George and I went in, and there was poor Aunt Udy, all laced up in that corset.

"It needs to be tighter. Here, George, hold this string. Ivy, you take this string and pull it as tight as you can." We did as we were told, and we got it all laced up.

"Now tie it, George, while Ivy and I hold it tight," said Mama.

George tied it, but instead of tying it in a bow knot, he tied it in a hard knot.

Aunt Udy put her dress back on to review the results. All of the fat was pushed up into her already ample bosom and down to her chubby thighs. This was not exactly the result Mama had expected.

"Walk around awhile, and see how you like it," said Mama.

"I already know how I like it," said Aunt Udy. "I don't! This thing is killing me! Now, get it off me," she said.

Mama said, "Give it a chance. I believe you may enjoy it."

Aunt Udy turned purple and shouted, "I said get this damn thing off me!" Nobody had ever heard Aunt Udy cuss before. She meant business!

Mama tried to untie the hard knot, but it held firm.

"George, why did you tie this in a hard knot?" she asked.

About that time, Uncle Joe Bob came in from the field. "What's going on in here?" He should have kept his mouth shut.

"You shut up, Joe Bob! If you wanted a slim woman, you should have married one! If you think I'm going to wear this thing, you are crazy!"

"What are you talking about, Judy?" Uncle Joe Bob didn't even know she had ordered a corset.

Aunt Udy started to cry. Uncle Joe Bob just stood there in a state of shock. He had never said he wanted a slender wife…he liked her cooking too much.

"Well, don't just stand there! Get me out of this!" said Aunt Udy.

"I can't," said Mama and Joe Bob at the same time.

"We're going to have to cut you out," said Mama.

"Then I can't send it back," said Aunt Udy.

Uncle Joe Bob said, "Please don't cry any more. We don't have to send it back."

"But it cost $5.95," said Aunt Udy.

"I don't care," said Uncle Joe Bob. "I'll use it in the barn. I can hoist calves up until they get steady on their feet."

We got the scissors and cut Aunt Udy out of that corset. She popped out everywhere.

For years to come, Aunt Udy's corset hung proudly in the barn. It was the best calf hoist Uncle Joe Bob ever had.

Chapter 17

Rachel

Mama collected stray people like other people pick up stray cats and dogs. Since she had such wonderful success with Mama June, she thought she might try her luck again.

Mama, Lucy, and Rachel had been best friends in college. Mama married Daddy when they were juniors in college. Lucy and Rachel graduated from college, and three years and a baby later, Mama went back to college and graduated. My Daddy went to war and got killed, and Mama and I lived with Mama June and Papa Jake.

After Lucy graduated from college, she married and got divorced six months later. Her "handsome prince" beat the shit out of her once. She moved out and never returned.

Rachel was a different story. Rachel married Clyde, but Clyde was lazy. Clyde wouldn't work, but Rachel worshiped Clyde…that is, until Mama and Lucy did an intervention on her.

Clyde didn't beat Rachel…he did much worse…he pecked away at her soul until she became his slave.

Clyde hated Mama and Lucy. He wouldn't let Rachel have lunch with Mama and Lucy, or go shopping with them. He said they were a "bad influence". Mama and Lucy hated Clyde even more than Clyde hated them, if that was possible.

Sometimes Rachel would slip off, when Clyde was on a weekend fishing trip with his buddies. She would tell Mama and Lucy what was going on in her life. Mama and Lucy were shocked at how Rachel looked and acted.

"I would visit more often," said Rachel, "but Clyde won't let me."

"Won't let you!?" exclaimed Lucy.

"Well, you know how much Clyde loves me," said Rachel. "He needs me so much. He won't eat anybody's cooking but mine."

Rachel looked awful. She was tired, her hair was long and stringy, she was as skinny as a rail, and she had no spirit. Rachel didn't even know herself how unhappy she was.

"I have to lay out his clothes for him," she said. "You know, he goes to church every Sunday. If he doesn't like what I've laid out, he takes the clothes to the clothes hamper, wads the up, and throws them in. I fix him ham and eggs every morning before I go to work. He wouldn't let me go to work until he lost his job."

"Shit!" Mama and Lucy cried together. They had heard enough.

George and I were listening to every word. We knew we might as well pack our suitcases...we were going to go somewhere.

Mama called Mama June and said, "I'm bringing Ivy and George to your house. I have to go out of town and I don't know how long I'll be gone.

Mama, Lucy, and Rachel got in the front seat of the car, and George and I got in the back seat. Rachel didn't know what was happening. George and I did...Rachel was being kidnapped!

Mama dropped George and me off at Mama June's house.

George and I were very nosy. We eventually found out everything about Mama's and Lucy's intervention and kidnapping.

After they left us at Mama June's house, Mama and Lucy drove Rachel straight to the Holiday Inn in Nashville and checked in.

Rachel was terrified. "Clyde'll kill me", she said.

"Well, he'll have to kill us, too," said Mama.

"It's about time you had a little fun," said Lucy. "I had a little taste of what you're going through, one time, and I sure do like my life better, now."

"You've got love mixed up with slavery," said Mama.

Actually, Clyde was like most of the men in Pea Ridge. They all thought they were right. The Holy Roller Preacher Man had told them, every Sunday, that the man is the head of the house...that is, until Mama, Lucy, and Papa Jake brought him to his knees. He would say, "The man is the head of the house, but don't let Anna and Lucy get hold of you!"

Every payday, Rachel would sign over her check to Clyde. He would give her a small amount of money and tell her what groceries to buy. He would dictate what he wanted to eat, and if it wasn't to his liking, he would take it to the back door and throw it out. "This ain't fittin' to eat," he would say.

Mama and Lucy together were people who got their way. Nobody wanted to mess with them. They loved Rachel and they were not about to let her be done wrong, even if Rachel *was* brainwashed. Mama and Lucy were determined to save her from the life she had gotten herself into.

"Walk a mile in my shoes and you'll never want to put yours on again," said Mama.

They called Mama June and told her they would be gone a week. It was summer vacation, and they had some free time.

Mama June said that she had a life, too, and she was taking George and me to Aunt Martha's. This was fine with us, because Aunt Martha was half crazy, and we could get away with just about anything.

After they checked in at the Holiday Inn, Lucy went out and bought a bottle of vodka, a bottle of vermouth, and a jar of olives. She proceeded to make martinis.

"I don't drink," said Rachel.

Lucy said, "You do now."

They drank and talked until three in the morning.

Martinis and two bitches is a dangerous combination. Rachel didn't have a chance. She was about to be enlightened.

"Anna, you used to be so sweet," said Rachel.

"I still am," said Mama. "I'm still a nice person. We just love you, and we don't want to see you treated like a dog."

"Rachel, we'll help you," said Lucy. "You just have to get out."

"Get out? Are you crazy? I love Clyde," said Rachel. "I'm calling Clyde right now.

As luck would have it, Clyde wasn't back from fishing. The phone rang and rang, until Rachel gave up.

Mama and Lucy knew that if they worked really hard, Rachel would break and everybody would be better off.

The next day, they slept until 11:00. Then, they had a big breakfast at the Waffle House that Rachel didn't have to cook.

"Please, please let me call Clyde to come and get me," pleaded Rachel, as she wrung her hands.

"No," said Mama. "It's out of your hands, now. There's nothing you can do."

They went to the same beauty shop that had worked miracles on Mama June. The stylist took a big handful of long, brown, stringy hair. Snip! And it was gone. She bleached, cut, and curled until Rachel's hair was beautiful. Then, the makeup artist took over. When she was done, Rachel was strikingly beautiful. She looked just like she did in college.

"Now," Lucy said, "we've got to get you out of those missionary clothes."

They drove to Harvey's and tried on clothes. Rachel had been very stylish in college. She had had all the right kind of clothes. Clyde had told her that it was a sin to dress like she did…it made men lust after her. One afternoon, he had taken all of her clothes out behind the house and burned them while Rachel was at the grocery store. When Rachel got back home, she didn't have any clothes, except the dress on her back.

Clyde went with her to the fabric store and he picked out some brown, black, and gray cloth. He told her that she had to go home and make some new clothes. Rachel was no seamstress, and she looked pitiful in her homemade clothes.

And now, with Mama and Lucy, Rachel was so brainwashed that she didn't even know how to pick out pretty clothes. When she went into Harvey's, the first thing she looked at was a black dress with a white collar.

Lucy chose a red sun dress and made Rachel try it on. Mama chose a yellow dress with a square neck and a straight skirt. Then, they went to the underwear department and bought Rachel a bra and some falsies.

"I'm not gonna wear falsies," said Rachel.

"Sometimes a girl needs a little help," said Lucy.

By the time they finished with her, Rachel was her old self again. She was confident, cute, and funny.

Rachel called Clyde and told him to go to hell, and that she wanted a divorce. He wasn't very happy about that, but eventually he gave in. Rachel was happy and much wiser.

Clyde moved back in with his aunt. She petted him and let him boss her around.

Chapter 18

▼

Princess

Forty-year-old Katherine Powers took one look at her perfect baby girl and said, "This is my little princess." That is what she called her…"Princess". George and I thought her name should have been *evil, wicked,* or *holy terror*. That was more appropriate. She was in our class every year, and we hated her. She called George "prissy" and she called me "red" or "fatso".

Princess and her mother gave Mama fits. Princess was lazy and she wouldn't do her homework. He mother did it for her. So, Princess would always turn in perfect papers. When Mama asked Katherine about it, she would lie and say that Princess was really smart, and that Mama just didn't realize it.

Princess was much fatter than I was. She had rotten teeth and huge black circles under her eyes. She loved to eat orange popsicles. Popsicle juice would run down her arm to her elbow. Her mother couldn't make Princess take a bath every day, so she went around with a long streak of orange down her arm. Her mother wouldn't make her comb her hair, either, and Princess would sleep in her clothes because she was too lazy to change them.

One time, Princess wound up in the hospital because she ate nothing but candy bars and orange popsicles for a whole month. Dr. Pooten was really mad at Katherine. "You have to make this child eat some vegetables, meats, and fruits," he said.

"She doesn't like vegetables, meats, and fruits," said Katherine.

"You're the mother! Make her!" said Dr. Pooten.

That day, when the nurse brought Princess her vegetable lunch, Princess threw it on the floor. Katherine said that it was an accident and she gave Princess a candy bar. Dr. Pooten had had enough.

"Well," he said, "if you won't eat right, then I am going to feed you intravenously. Nurse, let's get her hooked up."

You could hear Princess scream a mile away.

After two days of being fed through her veins, Princess decided that it might be easier to eat.

The poor nurses wouldn't go near her room. Katherine had to take care of her, night and day. Dr. Pooten sent her home after four days because he couldn't stand her, either.

Mama got to feeling sorry for Princess, because she had no friends. She told George and me that she thought it would be really nice if we would visit Princess one day after school. We said, "No way, we don't like her."

Mama tried guilt, because guilt usually worked. "You know that she just got out of the hospital," she said.

George and I said that we wished she was still in the hospital.

Mama said, "Aren't you ashamed of yourselves?"

"*No!*" we cried.

Mama would bend over backwards for her students, whether she liked them or not. She really was a good teacher, and she always said, "Happy students are good students."

None of the above worked. But she had something else up her sleeve that always worked…bribery.

"George and Ivy," she said, "I will buy you a cowboy and cowgirl outfit if you'll visit Princess for fifteen minutes after school."

This offer was too good to pass up. George and I had wanted cowboy outfits for the longest time. We wanted to wear them when we went skating. We could cut a rug on skates, and we were way too old to play cowboys.

After school one day, we walked to Princess' house. Princess' house was much bigger than our house, but not as big as Dr. Pooten's. Princess was a privileged child. Her parents owned the hardware store, and she had every toy you could ever imagine. I looked in her closet and it was full of beautiful clothes, matching shoes, and even hats. But at school, Princess dressed and looked like a poor child.

I loved her dolls, even though I had given up dolls a long time ago. I couldn't believe that Princess still played with dolls! She had one that opened and closed its eyes, and a Betsy Wetsy that would wet her diaper. George loved her games.

She had everything in the Sears and Roebuck catalog that we ever wanted. She even had a cowgirl suit!

We really wanted to play with Princess, but everything we touched; she started screaming, "*Put it down! Put it down! You are poor! You can't have things like mine! I'm rich!*

So, we said that maybe we should go home. Princess said that if we would stay, she would give us a Popsicle. We said, "O. K.". Princess got us a Popsicle out of the freezer. She got one for herself that had been in the refrigerator for about twenty minutes. Katherine always had Princess a Popsicle ready when she got home from school.

Well, you guessed it! George and I stuck the orange Popsicle in our mouths and our tongues got stuck. We tried to get them off, but they wouldn't budge. Then, our tongues started to hurt.

We started screaming, "*Dit it off! Dit it off!*" as best you can scream with a Popsicle stuck to your tongue. We were running around the house screaming "*Dit it off!*" when Katherine came in to see what was the matter.

"Don't you know better than to stick your tongue on a Popsicle straight out of the freezer?" she asked.

"*Dit it off*" we cried.

"Pull if off," said Princess.

"*It won't tome off,*" we cried even louder.

"Come over here to the sink," said Katherine. She poured R. C. Cola over our tongues until the Popsicles finally came loose. We threw them away and ran all the way home.

Princess did that on purpose. We were not only mad at Princess, but we were mad at Mama. So was Dr. Pooten.

"Anna," he said, "don't you ever make those children play with Princess Powers again. She's just *not right.*"

Chapter 19

Grandmother Gertrude Green

When Mama couldn't find anybody else to leave George and me with, when she went out of town with Dr. Pooten or Lucy, she would take us to Grandmother Green's house. This was a fate worse than death. George and I would get on our knees and beg Mama not to go, or at least, to let us stay home by ourselves.

First of all, Grandmother Green hated George and Mama, and she didn't exactly love me.

She was a very cold woman. She had a sour face and her nostrils flared when she was angry...which was all the time. She never hugged and kissed us. She was very critical and she called George a fuzzy-headed, prissy-assed bastard under her breath. She thought children should neither be seen *or* heard.

Gertrude thought she was better than us, and the only reason she tolerated us at all was because Big Daddy Green made her.

We overheard Mama telling Lucy the story of when she married my Daddy. She said that Gertrude went to bed for a year and tried to die. She made Kizzie Lou, her maid, bring all of her meals to her on a tray, and she only got up to go to the bathroom. She had a silver bell on a bedside table and when she rang it, Kizzie Lou had to run upstairs to wait on Gertrude. This drove Kizzie Lou crazy. When Gertrude realized, one day, that her pouting would not make Daddy leave

Mama and move back home with her and Big Daddy, she just got up and stayed up. She was cured!

Daddy was Gertrude's youngest son and the only person on earth that she truly loved. When Daddy was killed in World War II, she never got over it. She was even meaner than before. She was especially mean to Mama and George. She would ask Mama if she was still dating Dr. Farting. She knew Mama was sensitive about Dr. Pooten's name.

The only reason Mama would consider leaving us there was because of Big Daddy. He loved both me and Mama. He thought Mama was wonderful, and he loved me because I had his red hair. He loved George because Mama and I did. What Gertrude was missing, Big Daddy made up for. He was so good to us. He would buy us whatever we would ask for. He would let us do whatever we wanted to. He let us drive his Cadillac, and he took us to his farm so we could ride the horses. He let us run wild in the house and told Gertrude, when she complained of a headache, to go to bed and shut the door.

Hessie was Kissie Lou's daughter, and sometimes Hessie got to come to work with her. Grandmother Green would really throw a fit when that happened. George and I loved Hessie. She was a huge girl who wasn't afraid of anything! She took the best care of George and me.

Hessie said that Kissie Lou had worked for Mr. Green since the day he and Grandmother Green got married. She told us that Big Daddy didn't love Gertrude, but he had married her for her money…a decision he had regretted many a time. Big Daddy was very ambitious and marrying Gertrude was the fastest way for him to get money.

Big Daddy did, however, love his sons…my Daddy and Uncle Sonny.

Hessie said that Big Daddy had a girl friend, but I don't know about that. I do know that he spent a lot of time at his farm without Grandmother Green.

Grandmother Green fancied herself to be a socialite. She was raised that way. Big Daddy didn't fit in to that society because he, like Mama, said exactly what he thought.

One of our visits to Grandmother Green's especially stand out in my mind. George and I were about nine or ten years old, and Mama dropped us off to spend a few days at Grandmother Green's while she and Lucy went on a trip to choose textbooks for the next school year.

Grandmother Green was a member of the garden club. An elderly member, who was ninety years old, had died, and Grandmother Green made George and me go with her to the funeral. She made me put on a dress that she had bought for me. It was black, with a white collar. I was ten years old, for God's sake! I shouldn't have to wear black, even if it was to a funeral! Then, when she combed my curly red hair, she almost pulled me bald-headed. It hurt so bad that I cried, and that just made her mad, so she combed and pulled some more!

One of the ladies of the garden club got carried away with the funeral service, and she started crying hysterically. Her voice was quivering so loud that George and I got tickled. After all, the dead lady was ninety years old and we didn't know her, so we were not sad.

Then, another thing happened that made *us* hysterical. The preacher asked everybody to stand and sing a hymn. When the lady in front of us stood up, her dress got caught in her butt crack. George and I were laughing so hard that we had tears in our eyes. We had to pretend that we were crying, because people started to turn around and look at us. Grandmother Green glanced over at us and saw what was happening. She frowned and pinched a hunk out of each of us. It really hurt, and soon we were not pretending…we *were* crying!

The church ladies admired us for being such sensitive children…carrying on so over poor, dead Mrs. Roberts. Mrs. Roberts was a socialite, and Grandmother Green always wanted to be one, so she went to all of the socialite funerals.

We were invited to the family's home for dinner after the funeral. We knew we had better behave, or suffer more bruises from Grandmother's pinching.

Mrs. Robers' house was huge, with massive furniture. It was dark, and smelled old and rich.

The food wasn't very good…nothing like what we got at Dr. Pooten's house. I guess old, rich people can't cook much better than old, poor people. They should have had Kizzie Lou to cook for them. Now, Kizzie Lou can *cook*!

When we served our plates, George accidentally stepped on the butler bell, which was on the floor at the head of the table. An ancient black man in a threadbare black suit and a white ruffled shirt shuffled into the room and asked George, "Master Green, what do you need?"

George said, "Nothing", and the black man said, "Well, don't step on the butler bell no more unless you really need something."

When it was time for dessert, George and I chose banana pudding. It looked so tasty, and George and I were still hungry. When we put a big old spoonful in our mouth, it was *awful*! It was made out of milk from cows that had eaten wild onions!

We tried not to swallow the pudding. We were gagging, it was so bad. We had to figure out how to get rid of it. We eased over to a big old peace plant and dumped it in, and then we buried it in the potting soil.

We almost got by with the crime, except that George can't stand to have dirt on his hands, so he wiped them on the front of his white shirt. Grandmother Green was about to go into a rage over George's dirty white shirt when Big Daddy walked in (to show his respect for the dead, and to eat supper). This was a big mistake! He wasn't nearly as nice about the banana pudding as George and me.

"What's this shit?" he said, rather loudly, and spat a mouthful back in his bowl.

"George! Alice Ivy! This stuff is poison! Don't eat it!"

Grandmother Green was horrified. George and I were relieved…we didn't have to explain how George got dirt on his shirt.

Big Daddy got us out of there and took us over to the drug store to get ice cream. He left Grandmother Green there to smooth the ruffled aristocratic feathers.

Chapter 20

Shopping With Gertrude

I remember one time that Grandmother Green really did try to be nice to me. She took me shopping and to lunch in Nashville.

That whole day was such a disaster. The morning started off bad, even before we got in the car.

Grandmother Green was always trying to make me look the way *she* wanted me to look. I was planning to wear my overalls, but no…she made me wear a dress that she had bought for me. It looked like a holy roller's child's dress…big flowers, puffy sleeves, and a white collar. The next thing she did was to comb my hair. This almost killed me. She pulled half of it out, then made ringlets and put a big pink bow right on top of my head. When he saw me, George Washington laughed his head off!

I thought I might die if I had to wear that. I'll have to give her credit, though…I was told that I was pretty by one of her friends. That's the first time anyone had ever told me I was pretty, besides Mama and Big Daddy.

We shopped, and I didn't like any of the things that we bought. The thing I hated most was the wool riding habit. The legs stood out at the hips, making my chubby body look like two pigs in a poke trying to get out. Grandmother Green said that since I went to Big Daddy's farm to ride the horses, I needed a proper outfit. I had sat my fat butt on a horse only one time, and that was on old Getty-Up-Go, the old mare that was so slow that she would barely move.

I set about trying not to wear that riding habit before I ever got home. The damn thing cost over a hundred dollars, and I knew I'd have to have a good reason not to wear it.

Shopping was awful, but lunch was worse.

I wanted a hamburger and French fries at a drive-in. Grandmother Green would have no part of that. She said that proper people did not eat in the car. I said that Dr. Pooten was a proper person and that he took George and me to Pat's Drive-In anytime we wanted to go. This made her furious.

We went into a restaurant that had white table cloths and fresh flowers on the table. I said I wanted the lobster or the shrimp, but she ordered ham for both of us.

I wasn't that good using a knife at the table, and the ham was tough. I pressed down with the knife too close to the edge of the plate, and the whole plate flipped over. Peas and ham went everywhere, and my dress was a total mess. Carrots were in my shoes, and my white lace anklets were red from the Jell-O.

Grandmother Green paid the enormous bill, and we went to the ladies room to try to get me cleaned up. I was crying and I know Grandmother Green's blood pressure was sky high. I cleaned myself up the best I could, with her help. I took off my shoes and went bare foot. I tied my new sweater around my waist like an apron. That was the last time Grandmother Green ever took me shopping, and I thanked sweet Jesus for that.

When we got home, I had to try on that damn riding habit and show it to Big Daddy and George. Big Daddy said, "What in the hell is that, Gertrude? The child will look like a fool on Getty-Up-Go in that outfit, and she won't go near any of the other horses."

George thought I was the funniest thing he had ever seen. He was laughing and dancing around. I was ashamed of that riding habit, and I knew I would never wear it…although the hat wasn't bad.

That night I told George how bad I hated the riding habit. He said that sometimes Mama washes clothes when she needs clean underwear and doesn't want to wait for him to do the laundry. So, he said, just lay it on the floor in the washroom. Mama never separated clothes when she washed, and she always washed with hot water.

Well, the plan worked. I threw my riding habit on the floor of the washroom, and two weeks later, Mama needed some clean underwear. She threw everything that was on the floor in the washing machine and turned the water on hot. My wool riding habit came out of the washing machine the size of a doll dress.

Later, Grandmother Green asked me why she never saw me wearing my cute riding habit. When I showed it to her, she was really mad at Mama.

Chapter 21

Tent Meeting

As you already know, Mama wouldn't let me and George go to the Holy Roller church because we would have nightmares about going to hell.

The urge to go, though, was so strong that we couldn't help ourselves. There was a tent meeting going on within walking distance of our house. We could hear the music from the front porch.

We waited until Mama went to Dr. Pooten's house and we walked over to the tent meeting.

The music was good. George and I were singing, clapping our hands, and having a big old time. Then, all of a sudden, it happened. George screamed and started rolling on the ground. I didn't know what had happened.

The people in the tent went into a spiritual frenzy. "Praise God," they shouted, "the Holy Spirit has done entered the boy!"

One of the ladies fainted, and another one started speaking in tongues. The tent was really rocking.

By this time, a huge knot had popped up on George's nose.

"George, what happened to your nose," I whispered.

George was still whimpering. "I got wasp stung!"

"We'd better get out of here," I said.

We slipped out of the side of the tent and ran home. Mama wasn't back yet, so we went to bed.

We heard later that twenty or so souls were saved at the tent meeting. They got so loud that the sheriff had to break up the meeting.

The next day, George's nose was twice as large as it should be.

"What happened to your nose," Mama asked.

"I don't know," lied George.

"He slammed the car door on it," I said.

Mama knew we were both lying. She just couldn't figure out what *really* happened…or where we were when it happened.

Chapter 22

The Bandage

George liked to doctor everything. He once saved a chicken's life when it swallowed a piece of barbed wire. He operated on it, and that rooster was just fine for years to come.

A cat got run over in front of our house. George got Mama's vodka and some sugar in an eye dropper. He forced the cat to drink six dropper's full. The poor cat was so drunk that it passed right out. George went to work! He sewed up and set the cat's leg. Then, he said he needed a bandage.

I looked all over the house for something clean and sanitary. I finally found a huge bandage in the bottom of Mama's closet. The bandages were called Kotex and the box said they were sanitary. I looked around and found some string. George tied the bandage on the drunk cat.

George doctored that cat for two or three weeks, and lo and behold, it got well. One day the cat just walked off down the road. Actually, he looked a little funny. He walked slightly sideways and one eye was missing…but he lived.

Not long after that, George stepped on a rusty nail and I had to doctor him up. I didn't like it one bit, but George said I had to, or he might die of blood poisoning.

I got the vodka and George took a big swig. Then, I pulled the nail out and George screamed bloody murder. I gave George another big swig of vodka and then I poured some on the nail hole in George's foot.

I went and got another one of those Kotex sanitary bandages and tied it on George's foot. George said he didn't feel so good, and he thought he'd better go to bed.

The next morning, Mama went to school as she always did, and left George and me to get ready and come on later.

When we got to school, Lucy saw that George was limping, so she made him come in the office and sit down. This scared George and me to death.

When Lucy saw George's foot, she went and got Mama. She was laughing so hard she was snorting.

"Have you seen George this morning?" Lucy asked.

"No," said Mama. "Is he wearing that nylon stocking on his head again?"

"No," said Lucy, "but it's just as bad."

Mama looked George over and when she got to his foot she saw the Kotex on his foot.

"George, where did you get that?" she asked.

"Out of the bottom of your closet," he replied. "These are wonderful bandages. Ivy doctored my foot and it feels much better."

"We'd better take you to see Dr. Pooten," said Mama. "Lucy, I'll drop him off at the hospital and John can bring him back. George, I'll buy you some gauze and tape if you promise me you'll never use my Kotex for bandages again."

As Mama left the office, I saw her shaking with laughter. I didn't know what was funny until a few years later.

CHAPTER 23

▼

POISON IVY

I absolutely hated the song called "Poison Ivy". You guessed it! That became my name.

"Poison Ivy" was a good song to dance to, though. George and I could really dance. Mama taught us.

Nobel was the worst one to call me Poison Ivy. I knew I had to put a stop to that, and I did.

I was bigger than Nobel. I waited until we were changing classes one day. There was a big crowd in the hall, and Nobel said, "Here comes Poison Ivy."

I had my chance. "Look, you little son of a bitch," I said. "I haven't been called a name since I was in the fifth grade, and I don't have any intention of letting you start that again now."

I picked him up by the collar of his shirt. His feet came up off the floor and I scared the shit out of him. For the rest of our high school years, if he saw me coming, he would turn around and run the other way.

I was even with him again!!!

Chapter 24

Betty Sue

Instead of picking up stray animals and saving them, Mama saved stray people. That's the way we got George, and that's the way we got Betty Sue Eno.

Betty Sue Eno was a new teacher at Mama's school. Mama said that she had the potential to be a wonderful teacher. She was very dedicated to her students, and she worked so hard. Mama would help her with her problems, and in a short time, they became friends.

One day, Betty Sue didn't come to work. Mama called her to see what was wrong. Betty Sue said she was a little under the weather, but she would be back to school the next day. Well, the next day Betty Sue came back and she was black and blue all over. She had been beat up.

Mama had had experience in dealing with abusive husbands, remembering how she and Lucy had saved Rachel. Mama told Betty Sue that she was coming home with us.

Of course, Betty Sue objected. She said that she loved Buddy and she didn't want to leave.

Mama said, "Buddy doesn't love you. People don't hit other people they love!"

Betty Sue stayed with us for a month, long enough to know how it felt not to be beat up. Buddy came to our house and begged Betty Sue to come home with him. Mama ran him off. He came to school to see Betty Sue, and Lucy called her cousin, the sheriff.

Rumors were going around the school that Buddy was having a fling with a loose girl, nineteen years old. They drank a lot, and Buddy often passed out in the yard.

George and I were in the ninth grade. We had been driving cars, trucks, and tractors since we were in the fourth grade. Papa Jake had taught us how to drive when we were helping him haul hay.

We "borrowed" Mama's car…actually, we stole it. One midnight, we crawled out the window and pushed the car down the driveway. We drove past Betty Sue's house, and sure enough, Buddy was passed out cold, lying in the yard.

George and I know exactly what we were going to do. We had read it in a country music artist magazine. Somebody's wife had sewn him in a sheet and beat the shit out of him with a broom.

We had our own sheet in the car, and needles and thread. We got out of the car and cautiously rolled Buddy onto the sheet. He groaned a little, but he didn't wake up because he was really passed out.

We sewed as fast as we could, until the job was done. At the last minute we decided we would transport him to Roty Fitz's house. We drove Mama's car into Betty Sue's yard, and we lifted and tugged until we finally got Buddy in the car. We prayed real hard that the law wouldn't catch us.

We drove carefully with our drunken cargo until we got to Roty's house. We rolled Buddy out in the yard and then we got the hell out of Dodge.

We drove home and slipped in the house. Fortunately, Mama and Betty Sue didn't wake up.

Rumors travel fast in small towns. We heard the ending of the story the next day at school. Nobody ever knew that George and I were involved.

This is what we heard: Buddy woke up after we rolled him out of the car, and he somehow managed to get up to Roty's porch. He was screaming, "I'm blind and I'm crippled. Help me! *Help me!*"

Roty came to the door and looked out on the porch. She saw what she thought was a ghost, and she started running through the house hollering, "Lord, cleanse me of my sins. I shouldn't have gone out with a married man. The Angel of Death has come to get me!"

This woke up her parents. They thought Roty was having a nervous breakdown. They went out the back door with Roty, got her in the car, and drove her to the emergency room. They never saw Buddy sewn up in the sheet on the front porch.

Roty was screaming, so when they got her to the hospital, Dr. Pooten thought she was out of her head. She was talking about "haints" coming to carry her away to the bosom of Abraham and about being a sinner for going out with a married man.

Buddy eventually got out of the sheet and realized he wasn't blind or crippled. Roty stayed in the mental ward of the hospital for five days. When she got out, she became a missionary and moved to China, devoting her life to the Lord.

Buddy was so humbled by the whole experience that he gave Betty Sue the divorce she wanted. He moved back to his home town in Alabama.

George and I never got caught. Betty Sue soon got back on her feet and moved on with her much improved life.

Chapter 25

The Yankees Are Coming! The Yankees Are Coming!

They came down every year in June and stayed two long, long weeks. We always dreaded the invasion of the Yankee kin. Gordon Ezra was Papa Jake's brother, and he brought his wife Eunice, and his teenage children, Rocky and Cricket, with him.

Gordon Ezra worked in the Ford plant in Detroit, Michigan.

We helped Mama June get ready for them. We changed sheets, painted, polished, bought new linens and stocked up on food. Mama June no longer liked to cook and clean, but she would do this to please Papa Jake.

For two weeks we put up with the abuse and the insults. None of us were excused from it. A typical conversation went like this:

"Jake, why don't you get a real job? Farm work don't pay no money," said Gordon Ezra. "I can get you on at the plant up in Detroit."

"June, why do you drive a Cadillac?" asked Gordon Ezra. Mama June's car was her pride and joy.

"She thinks she's better than us," said Aunt Eunice.

"How many miles to the gallon does that car get? It's a gas guzzler, isn't it?" Gordon Ezra asked.

"You'se guys talk funny, don't you?" said Cricket.

"Don't you got no pop? I don't like ice tea," said Rocky.

Eunice put in another two cents worth. "It's a shame Anna's not more like Mattie. Mattie's got her a man and her children are so sweet. Can't you find a man to marry you, Anna?"

They all loved Aunt Mattie and told us how wonderful she was. George, Mama, and I couldn't stand whiney-butt Mattie.

Eunice wouldn't help Mama June with the cooking or cleaning. She said she was on her vacation. She sat on the front porch and read *True Story* and *True Confession* magazines. She also complained a lot. To top it all off, she asked Mama June to hem her dress. Mama June didn't want to, but she did it anyway.

Cricket spilled a whole bottle of fingernail polish on Mama June's brand new chenille bedspread.

Rocky sat a bottle of R. C. Cola down on Mama June's sideboard and made a white ring on it.

Aunt Eunice asked Mama why she didn't dye my red hair black. This was almost the last straw. Mama loved my red hair, and she was not big on keeping in her thoughts.

"Why don't you dye Cricket's hair red?" asked Mama. "An even better idea would be for you to make her wash the nasty mess."

Uncle Gordon Ezra and his family took Aunt Mattie and her family to Rock City, and didn't take us. They weren't going to tell us they went, but Aunt Mattie's station wagon had a "See Rock City" sign on the bumper. King said they didn't want us to go because we're so uppity.

Cricket spent one night with me. While she was at our house, she got into Mama's closet without asking and she put on Mama's favorite blouse. She was larger than Mama, and she popped two buttons off. Then, she pinned it up with a safety pin.

Mama loved her clothes as much as Mama June loved her Cadillac. Mama held her temper cool until Cricket left. Then, she threw the blouse on the floor, stomped it, and then she threw it in the trash.

Mama did make one more feeble effort to be nice. She told George and me to take the car and ride Rocky and Cricket around town.

George and I were cute, and we had lots of friends by the time we were in high school. We picked up Mabeline and Wiley to ride around with us. Rocky said Mabeline would look alright, if she had some knockers. Mabeline overheard him. It hurt her feelings and she cried.

One of the few things Mama and Mama June completely agreed upon was that they both intensely disliked Uncle Gordon Ezra, Aunt Eunice, and their rude teenagers.

The visit was finally coming to an end, and Papa Jake wanted to have a farewell dinner for them. Mama June reluctantly agreed to it, if George, Mama, and I would help her with the cooking. We said we would do whatever it took to get rid of them.

Mattie said she was sick and couldn't help; however, she came and sat on the porch with Eunice, and they both read *True Story* magazines.

We got there early on a Saturday morning and started to work. We brought Lucy with us. You know what a great cook George was, so he mixed up one of his famous chocolate cakes. Mama was peeling potatoes, Lucy was snapping beans, and I was making my delicious Jell-O.

Uncle Gordon Ezra walked through the hot kitchen and said, "I can't eat none of this stuff. Don't ya'll have any Spam?"

George had on his "Kiss The Cook" apron when Rocky came through the kitchen. He started laughing and pointing at George.

"George, are you a sissy or are you a prissy butt? I looove your apron," he teased, dragging out the word "love".

Sweet, non-violent George exploded. He picked up that bowl of chocolate cake batter and turned it upside down on Rocky's greasy head. Cake batter dripped all the way down to his shoes. He ran crying out of the kitchen. "I'm telling Daddy," he wailed.

When he was gone, we started clapping, "Way to go, George!" George calmly got out another bowl and started mixing another cake.

Dr. Pooten came for supper that night. When we sat down to eat, Uncle Gordon Ezra said, "I work in the Ford plant. What do you do, John?"

"I'm a doctor," said Dr. Pooten.

"Anna, you're getting mighty uppity, aren't you, having a *doctor* for a friend?" asked Uncle Gordon Ezra. "Pooten...that's a funny name. Are you a foreigner?"

"No," said Dr. Pooten.

"We ought to call him Dr. Farting, shouldn't we Dad?" laughed Rocky.

"That's a funny one son, Farting," Uncle Gordon Ezra chuckled.

"Rocky, are you a boil on the butt of humanity?" asked Mama, who was very sensitive about Dr. Pooten's name.

Mama, Mama June, and Lucy had had enough. George and I knew the shit was going to hit the fan.

Mama stood up. "Uncle Gordon Ezra, why don't you get your lazy wife and your rude children and your fat ass in your Ford and take yourself back to Michigan where you belong?"

"Now, Anna," said Dr. Pooten

"No," Mama June said, "Anna's right. We've gone out of our way to be gracious. Now, I've got something to give you…take this damn Spam with you!"

Lucy added, "Don't let the door hit you in the butt on your way out."

It would be years before we would see Uncle Gordon Ezra and his family again. I can't say that any of us were unhappy about that.

Chapter 26

Mabeline Lewis

Mabeline Lewis had the best figure in the whole class of 1960. She was tall and had long, shiny hair, and she had the biggest boobs you ever saw.

I was so flat chested that I think I could have passed for a boy if I needed to. Mabeline had perfect boobs and she liked to show them off in tight sweaters.

George Washington said he was pretty sure they weren't real. I said they were, and George said that on some days, they were bigger than on other days.

Mabeline's parents owned the clothing store in town, so she put on airs. If she had acted as nice as she looked, the unfortunate incident that took place might never have happened.

I don't know if what happened ruined Mabeline's life or not, but after the incident, she turned out to be almost sweet to George and me.

You see, Mabeline was a cheerleader, and all of the cheerleaders hung around together. They thought they were better than the rest of the girls in the class.

On a Friday afternoon in October we were having a pep rally for the football team, and everybody was in the gym. Mabeline was jumping up and down when the tragedy happened. Her bra broke, and two pair of rolled-up socks came tumbling out from under her letter sweater.

Everybody started laughing and cheering. I felt really bad for her, but she had been so mean to less fortunate people in the past, that on the other hand, she kind of deserved it. Once, I overheard her saying to a poor girl, "Can't you dress any better than that? You wear the same outfit every other day!"

Mabeline ran out of the gym, crying. She stayed home for a week, until Lucy sent Mama over to talk to her and get her back in school. Mama took George and me with her, but we wouldn't get out of the car.

Mama stayed in Mabeline's house for about an hour, and then she came out. She made George and me come in, saying that Mabeline wanted to give us a Coke. Mabeline was actually nice to us. I couldn't believe it.

Mabeline was crying. "I'll never have another friend," she wailed.

"Alice Ivy and George will be your friends," said Mama. "You can count on them."

George and I looked at each other. We had been the victim of Mabeline more times than we could count. Now, she acted like she was doing us a big old favor.

"Sure," Mabeline said.

Mama said that we had to go and that she would see Mabeline in class tomorrow.

The next day, Mabeline showed up at school, and her sweater was as flat as a pancake.

I don't know how it happened, but nobody ever teased her. I guess she was just used to being treated better than everybody else. However, from that time on, she was much nicer to George and me.

Chapter 27

Something Just Ain't Right

Wilson Gann was the meanest jerk in our class, and that is saying a lot, because our class had some really mean jerks. Maybe the reason Wilson was so mean was because his Mama spoiled him and his Daddy whupped him.

When Wilson was four years old, his Mama was canning tomatoes. Wilson pulled a pot of boiling tomatoes off the stove and they scalded his left arm. His Mama bent his elbow and wrapped his arm up in a bandage. Wilson would cry real hard when she tried to straighten his arm and doctor it, so she left it bent far too long. His arm grew together like a web-footed duck. Wilson was never able to straighten his arm out after that.

Wilson didn't have many friends. Almost everybody was afraid of him. He made everybody pay for that arm…especially George and me.

There are a lot of mean people in the world, and it seemed like we had the majority of them in our class.

George and I were smart, and that made all the mean people mad at us. We didn't have to do anything to provoke them…they just didn't like us.

There were two sets of twin boys in our class, and I don't know which set was the meanest…Big'un and Big'un's brother, or Worthy and Nobel.

Worthy and Nobel were anything but worthy and noble. They would lie and steal without even batting an eye. Not only were they mean as snakes, but they were ugly and stupid.

Their mother died giving birth to them. They were raised…somewhat…by their mean and stupid father. George and I felt sorry for them before we became their victims.

They stole our pencils and lied about it; they borrowed our crayons, broke them, and lied. They stole our markers, lied, and said the markers were theirs. They stuck bubble gum in my hair and I had to get it cut out, and this left a big gap in my hair.

Nobel farted in class and blamed it on me.

"Alice Ivy farted," said Nobel.

Everybody laughed and pointed at me.

"*Did not!*" I said, and I started crying.

I hated Worthy and Nobel.

Worthy tied George's shoe strings together and George fell flat on his face. Nobel tied George to his chair, and George and his chair fell flat on his face.

Nobel stole my homework, erased my name, and turned it in as his.

They did not bathe or brush their teeth; they smelled bad, and had bad breath.

Eventually Wilson, Worthy, and Nobel got what was coming to them. We had already dealt with Big'un and Big'un's brother.

We almost killed them, but now it was time to deal with them.

Chapter 28

A Man's Got to Do What a Man's Got to Do

George Washington and I were the best skaters you ever saw. We practiced all the time at the Roll-A-Round Roller Rink.

We saved our money to get matching outfits…satin shirts for both of us (George loved his and wanted to wear it all the time)…and a short skirt for me, and flowing, soft pants for George. We had to get Mama June to make George's pants. We couldn't find any like we wanted in the stores. We even went to Nashville, and the closest thing we could find cost $25.00…way too much for our budget.

I must admit that we showed out all the time, skating backwards, swaying back and forth, skating to the music. My favorite music to skate to was "Down Yonder" and "Bonaparte's Retreat" because they had such a good beat. George's britches just puffed out and flowed because we went so fast.

Wilson Gann hated George Washington because he thought George was a sissy, I guess. We tried to never be at the Roll-A-Round when Wilson was there, but occasionally we had to share the floor with Wilson. Well, this one time, Wilson was there, and this is what happened.

Wilson came out of nowhere, stuck his foot out, and tried to trip George Washington. But, like I said, we were excellent skaters. Wilson fell flat on his face, knocked himself out, and bloodied his own nose.

I had to think fast. I knew Wilson would want to murder George when he woke up. I started shouting, "George, why did you bloody Wilson's nose?" George and I were close by this time, and we could read each other's thoughts.

"Well, the son-of-a-bitch kept calling me 'sissy', and I just got tired of it," he said.

Nobody except George and I knew exactly what happened. When Wilson started coming to, a crowd had gathered around Wilson. People in the crowd told Wilson that George Washington had hit him and bloodied his nose.

From that day on, Wilson had a healthy respect for George Washington. He left George alone and never called him a sissy again. Almost everybody else stopped teasing George, too, because if he bloodied Wilson Gann's nose, George would surely do the same thing to them.

Chapter 29

▼

Red Man Blues

Mama was a very generous woman, especially with Dr. Pooten's money. All she had to do was ask, and Dr. Pooten would pull out a big roll of money. He would ask Mama how much she needed, and start peeling off some bills. Mama usually needed a lot.

Mama was having trouble with Worthy and Nobel in her class. She decided it was probably because they had no decent clothes to wear to school. She could take care of that problem! She got a big wad of money from Dr. Pooten and went shopping for Worthy and Nobel. Then, to our absolute horror, she invited them over to our house one Saturday for lunch.

We had no use for Worthy and Nobel! We told Mama that we wanted to go visit Aunt Martha, but Mama would have no part of that. She always used guilt first, and if that didn't work, she moved on to bribery. George and I held out for bribery.

"I want you two to be nice to Worthy and Nobel," she said. "They don't have a Mama, and their Daddy's a snake in the grass."

George and I said that they were never very nice to us.

Mama's bribery was that George didn't have to fix lunch, and she took us shopping, too.

George didn't want to cook, but he knew that leaving lunch to Mama was a big mistake. George and I knew what lunch was going to be…Spam on a long stick (kabobs, Mama called them) with olives stuck on a toothpick in each slice of meat. For dessert, we would have marshmallows with red and green maraschino cherries on a toothpick. stuck in the marshmallow.

For our part in being host and hostess to Worthy and Nobel, George and I got to go to a movie in Nashville, a new jigsaw puzzle each, and a badminton set.

When the Saturday for the visit came around, Worthy's and Nobel's daddy dropped them off at our house. They were in the bed of the pickup truck, hollering and pushing each other. When they got in our yard, they jumped out and ran in our house. In five minutes, they had our new puzzle pieces all mixed up, and the birdie in our badminton set was torn up.

Mama persisted in her crusade, and gave them each new blue jeans, shirts, shoes, and socks.

"Much obliged," they mumbled. They went upstairs to change, and after they came back, they looked and acted nice for about five minutes.

Then, it was time for lunch. Sure enough, Mama made her spam-kabob-with-an-olive-on-a-toothpick lunch and she served it on our good dishes. Worthy and Nobel had never eaten an olive before, and they didn't like them, so they spit them back on Mama's china. Mama didn't like that one bit!

"Ya'll go on out to the porch, now. I'll bring dessert out there. Sure enough, Mama had marshmallows-with-maraschino cherries-on-a-toothpick for dessert.

"When is your daddy going to pick ya'll up?" asked Mama.

"He said we could stay here a long time," said Nobel.

"Well, ya'll go down to the woods and identify trees and birds. Write down the name of each one you see, and bring me a leaf off of each tree."

We started off to the woods, but Worthy and Nobel said that girls weren't allowed. It was a boy's only field trip. But, I followed them anyway, hiding behind trees. I figured George was going to need some help. Before they were even out of sight, Worthy pulled out a slingshot and popped George in the butt!

As soon as they were deep in the woods, Nobel pulled out a bag of Red Man chewing tobacco out of his pocket. He teased George until George took a big plug of it and started to chew on it. George was trying very hard to get along with them. I was hiding where I could see the whole thing.

George chewed awhile, and then he swallowed the plug. Then, he took another plug and chewed some more, and he swallowed that, too.

Worthy and Nobel were dancing around, bent over with laughter. They thought it was so funny that George had gotten to be as big as he was and never had chewed any tobacco.

About that time, George started turning pale and did a projectile throw-up. It got all over Worthy's and Nobel's new clothes and shoes. They both balled up their fists to sock George, and as they did, George let go of another round again, all over them. They were covered, from head to toe, with throw-up, and they were furious.

I knew it was time for me to step in. I jumped from behind a tree and yelled, "Run, George, run!" Six foot, six inch George could really run when he had to…but he always ran with his eyes closed. He was kicking up dust, trying to get away from Worthy and Nobel, but he was headed straight for a tree.

I hollered, "To the right, George, to the right!"

George turned and barely missed the tree, but Nobel wasn't so lucky. He hit the tree, addled himself, and hit the ground.

Worthy screamed, "Now see what you've done. You've gone and killed my brother! You'll pay for this!"

"He's not dead," I yelled back. "He's just knocked a little woozy. He'll be alright."

By this time, George was feeling a little better, and he didn't have a speck of throw-up on him.

"We'd better get Nobel to Mama," I said.

Nobel couldn't walk straight, so Worthy and George propped him up between them and helped him to walk.

I have already mentioned that Worthy and Nobel would steal anything that wasn't tied down.

Pretty soon, three dogs came out of nowhere and started circling around us. They began to get more aggressive and jumped up on the boys.

"They smell the Spam," said Worthy.

"Give it to them," mumbled Nobel.

Worthy and Nobel had stolen some of the Spam off of Mama's kabobs and put it in their pockets. Worthy started to run and pull the meat from his pockets at the same time. The dogs were right behind them, nipping at Worthy's and Nobel's legs.

"Give them the Spam!" hollered George.

Worthy started throwing Spam at the dogs. This calmed them down a little bit, but they still followed us all the way home.

Mama came outside to see what all the racket was about. She took one look at Worthy and Nobel and asked, "What's going on here?"

None of us were about to tell her the truth. "We got sick on them olives," Nobel lied.

"That pack of wild dogs tried to kill us," said George.

"Nobel stepped on his shoe string. He fell down and hit his head," I continued.

"I'm sorry…we didn't get to identify any trees," said George.

Mama dug Worthy's and Nobel's old clothes out of the garbage can. "Go behind the house," she told them, "and put these clothes back on. I'll take your new ones inside to wash them."

George went with her to make sure she didn't wash the clothes in hot water and make them shrink.

Worthy and Nobel did as they were told, but they were crying…just weeping and wailing.

George and I felt a little sorry for them, but that didn't last long. After all, we thought about all the mean things they had done to us. I guess we were even!

Worthy's and Nobel's daddy drove up about that time.

"Woman," he yelled. "What have you done to my boys? Just look at 'em! They're filthy, and Nobel's got a knot on his head! You need a whuppin'!" Worthy's and Nobel's daddy used to go to the Holy Roller church to hear Preacher Man.

"Shut up and get back in that truck, or I'll beat you so you look worse than them!" she exclaimed. Their daddy knew Mama's reputation from when she dealt with Preacher Man, and he didn't want any part of that. He jumped back in the truck, and Worthy and Nobel climbed up in the truck bed. They peeled rubber to get away from Mama.

The next day, Mama took Worthy's and Nobel's clean clothes over to their house. They loved Mama after that, and they started acting better in class. And, they left George and me alone.

Chapter 30

Bird Houses and Chocolate Pie

As you already know, George Washington and I were both smart. George was smarter than me, though. We would study together every night. George hardly ever made lower than 100 on anything…with one big exception: Wood Shop! George couldn't hit a nail on its head to save his life, and he made an "F" on his bird houses. This nearly killed him.

George begged to do it over, and sweet Mr. Trueblood let him. Mama and I built that bird house for George and he made a "B-minus" on it.

George really wanted to take Home Economics, rather than Wood Shop, but Miss Emma Jean Hollowell wouldn't let him. She said that boys weren't supposed to cook. George loved to cook. He did all of our cooking, and this hurt George's feelings. Every day, George would ask me what we did in Home Economics that day.

George was starting to grow up and he wasn't nearly as prissy as he had been.

I didn't like Miss Emma Jean very much. She was very haughty. She kept making me do stuff over, like cook something again, or pick out the stitches on my apron.

I knew for sure that I wasn't going to be a housewife, so I didn't see any need to learn all that stuff.

The worst thing Miss Emma Jean ever made us do was to enter a dish in the county fair. There were four categories…main dish, bread, dessert, and salad. I quickly signed up for dessert. I was going to enter Jell-O. I knew I could make Jell-O because I made it all the time. My Jell-O was the best stuff I had ever tasted and it was easy to do. Just a box of Jell-O, a can of fruit cocktail, and a handful of miniature colored marshmallows.

At that time, Jell-O was new to our little town. I loved the way it wiggled and how pretty it was.

Miss Emma Jean would have no part of my plan to enter Jell-O. "First of all," she said, "Jell-O is a salad, it's not a dessert, and all of the salad spots have been taken."

I argued with her, and it made her as mad as a wet hen, so she assigned me chocolate pie to make.

I had never made a chocolate pie in my life. I was really mad at her, but I had no choice.

I went home and went to work on my pie. It turned out to be worse than awful. The crust was soggy and it had a big hole in it. The filling scorched and it was lumpy. But the meringue was the worst. It was as flat as a flitter.

George came home from basketball practice and started making fun of it, so I started to cry.

"What am I going to do?" I wailed.

George felt sorry for me and he said he would help me. After I fumbled around in the kitchen for a little while, George sent me outside, so I practiced my skating on the sidewalk. George didn't just help me…he did it himself! He made the most beautiful chocolate pie, with a light brown crust and fluffy meringue.

I proudly entered that pie in the county fair contest. To my horror, my pie won. I didn't want it to win…I just wanted to pass Home Economics.

The judges gathered around me.

"I taste something a little different in your filling," said one judge.

Another judge said, "That pie's good enough to make a Baptist dance."

"Will you tell us your secret ingredient?" asked a third judge.

I had to think fast. "Lemon," I blurted out.

"*Lemon*! Are you sure?" they asked.

"Yep, it's lemon. Just put a little lemon in the milk, and blend it into the filling," I said.

Miss Emma Jean didn't like me much in the first place, but after the pie incident, she really hated me. You see, she was having the preacher over for Sunday dinner, and she made my chocolate pie recipe. The lemon, of course, curdled the milk, and the pie couldn't be eaten. Miss Emma Jean had to serve Jell-O for dessert.

Later on, I asked George what he had put in that pie to make it so good. He said that he just sprinkled a little cinnamon in the filling.

I barely made a "C" in Home Economics, and I only got it because Mama went and talked with Miss Emma Jean. Miss Emma Jean gave me extra assignments.

It didn't hurt that Mama was Lucy's best friend, and Lucy was the school principal. I don't think Lucy liked Miss Emma Jean too much better than I did.

Chapter 31

George Makes the Basketball Team

The only way I could persuade George Washington to try out for the basketball team was to tell him he would get to wear those little satin shorts. George didn't like to run, he didn't like to sweat, and he especially didn't like to get his hair messed up.

The basketball coach disliked George right off, because George was smarter than the coach.

The basketball coach wasn't going to let George be on the team, until Lucy made him. She said, "Watch what George can do. Shoot, George."

George threw the ball at the hoop and *swish*...in went the ball.

"Stand over here, shoot," Lucy said. *Swish* went the ball through the hoop.

"Over here," she said. *Swish*!

Every time, from anywhere on the court, the ball swished through the hoop. George was good!

George said he would play, but he wasn't going to run or sweat. The coach said he didn't care. George didn't have to do any of that...he could just stand there and make baskets. Coach knew he was going to have a winning team.

George had had a growing spurt. He had grown to fit his teeth. He was six feet, six inches tall.

"By the way, coach," said Lucy, "I want George to do your attendance register every day. I want it done right for a change."

Everybody was happy. George got to wear satin without people making fun of him. The coach had a winning season. And Lucy didn't have to re-do the coach's attendance register. It was right every month.

Chapter 32

Florida or Bust

Aunt Mattie invited George and me to go on a family vacation to Florida.

I said I didn't want to go because I hated Aunt Mattie and her family, but George had always wanted to go to Florida, and he wouldn't go without me. He knew our cousins would gang up on him, and he needed me along to be on his side.

The only reason Aunt Mattie invited us to go is because she wanted Mama to pay for half the trip. Mama reluctantly agreed to do this.

I think Mama really wanted George and me to go on the trip so she could have some time alone with Dr. Pooten.

She told us we could buy new clothes for the trip. George loved clothes almost as much as he loved doctoring things.

Mama took us to Nashville to spend the day shopping, a week before our trip.

George was in Heaven. He bought new blue jeans, a madras shirt, new shorts, new T-shirts, putter pants, bathing trunks, and blue suede shoes.

I got a new can-can, garter belt, a straight skirt, a gathered skirt, pedal pushers, and a sun dress. We also got new luggage. Mama made us get that. George and I said we would rather have more clothes. We said we could pack in a box or a paper bag, but, as usual, Mama won the argument.

George and I were cute teen-agers. We were both sixteen. George had grown to fit his teeth and I had slimmed down. George was six feet, six inches tall.

Mama took us to Harvey's in Nashville to buy us some high quality clothes. We bought part of our clothes there, but we both insisted that we go to another, cheaper store, where our money would go farther. Mama said we would be sorry. (She was right, as we would find out!)

The day before the trip, George and I went to the Piggly Wiggly and bought our favorite food…bologna sausage, cheese, soda crackers, Mallo-Mars, Goo-Goo Clusters, Moon Pies, Vienna sausage, grapes, and bananas. We came home and George made teacakes and brownies while I made sandwiches…bologna sausage and mustard on light bread. We put it all in a large paper bag. Florida was looking pretty good after all.

We were packed and ready to go, against my better judgment. I didn't like anybody who was going down to Florida except George Washington, although sometimes, Uncle Pud was O. K.

Mama said she was going to Nashville to a teacher's convention, but George and I knew she and Dr. Pooten were going on a trip. We had heard them planning it.

George and I made a sign that said, "Florida or Bust", and then we put film in our Brownie camera.

We were in bad trouble before we got out of Pea Ridge…as a matter of fact, before we even got out of our driveway. Aunt Mattie had brought Cupcake, her big, ill-tempered dog along. I couldn't believe that, but I should have known! She loved Cupcake better than she loved her own children.

While George and Uncle Pud were tying our suitcases on top of Uncle Pud's 1957 turquoise station wagon, I put the "Florida or Bust" sign in between the "Honk If You Love Jesus" and "See Rock City" signs.

Cupcake got a whiff of George's and my food bag. By the time I noticed what was happening, she had eaten all of the bologna sausage sandwiches, and all of the cheese and crackers. She had gnawed at the bananas and she had slobbered on the grapes. All that was left of our food was the Goo-Goo Clusters and the Malo-Mars. Aunt Mattie had George's tea cakes and brownies in the front seat, eating them.

We should have stayed home. Things went downhill from there.

Roger and King sat in the back seat, and they made George sit in the middle. Now this is about impossible, since George had now grown to be over six feet. Roger and King *had* to have a seat by the window, though, so George just had to do the best he could. Rose and I sat in the very back, while Cupcake jumped from one seat to the other.

There was no air conditioning in the car, and it was the middle of July. Aunt Mattie wouldn't roll down her window because she didn't want to mess up her hair. My expensive hair-do was already a kinky mess.

We pulled out of the driveway at 8:00 in the morning, and by 9:00, King had to go to the bathroom.

Uncle Pud was a tiny man and most of the time he was quiet and nice, but when he got behind the wheel of a car, he turned into a maniac.

He wheeled the car to a quick stop and told King to get out and go pee behind a tree. Uncle Pud wanted to make good time.

After King relieved himself, he got back in the car and Uncle Pud started flying down the road again. We didn't have seat belts in the car, so on every curve, we bounced into each other.

Aunt Mattie started asking questions about Mama.

"Alice Ivy, what's Anna Ronda going to do while ya'll are gone?"

"She's going to a teacher's convention," I lied.

"*H'ump*! I'll bet she is! She's going to sleeze around with John Pooten," she said. "I'll bet they're going on a trip. Everybody knows she's whoring around with him!"

"My Mama's not whoring around," George said.

"She's not your Mama, anyway," said Aunt Mattie.

"Is too," I said, "and why do you have to talk about her so mean?"

"She ought to marry him," said Aunt Mattie. "Her carrying on embarrasses me to death! I'm a good, Christian woman, and my own sister's carrying on like a concubine!"

"Take me back home!" I said. "I won't listen to any more lies about my Mama!"

"We will not! Why are you trying to mess things up for everybody?" Aunt Mattie asked. "We're too far down the road, now, to turn around."

"Cupcake is farting in my face," said Rodger.

"My sweet Cupcake doesn't do such things. Stop doing that, Pud!" said Aunt Mattie.

It never ceased to amaze me that Aunt Mattie is Mama's sister. They are nothing alike. Mama is beautiful, tall, and blonde. Aunt Mattie is plain and verging on ugly. Mama is funny, sweet, and kind. Aunt Mattie is mean, narrow minded, and very jealous of Mama. Mama got all of Papa Jake's and Mama June's good qualities. Aunt Mattie got everybody in the family's bad features, and on top of that, she's sickly.

We went along being quiet for a while, and then we stopped along side the road at a picnic table to have lunch. Aunt Mattie got their lunch out, and it was awful: cold meat and biscuits left over from breakfast, cold corn bread, and sweet potatoes left over from supper. I was starving, but I wasn't eating that stuff!

"Mattie, what on earth is this mess," asked henpecked Pud.

"I was trying to save us some money," whined Aunt Mattie.

George and I ate our Mallo-Mars and shared a Goo-Goo Cluster. We felt sorry for King, Rodger, and Rose, so we gave them our other Goo-Goo Cluster to share. Cupcake had fried chicken.

Back in the car again, everything went along smoothly until we came to Marietta, Georgia. Traffic there was awful. Uncle Pud got really tense and gripped the steering wheel until his knuckles were white. When traffic came to a halt, he sat down on the horn. Of course, there was no place for the cars in front of us to go. The horn blowing made the big man in front of us mad. He got out of his car, came back to the station wagon, and told Uncle Pud to get out of the car. Uncle Pud, at five feet, four inches, got out. The man grabbed him by the shirt collar and picked him up off the road. Lucky for Uncle Pud, six feet, six inch George got up his courage and got out of the station wagon. He told the big man to put Uncle Pud down. The man took one look at George, apologized, and got back in his car.

We started moving again, but Uncle Pud was in the wrong lane. We wound up in downtown Atlanta, going around and around the Capitol Building of Georgia. After we went around the block about six times, George said we needed to pull over and ask directions. Uncle Pud would have no part of that.

George asked Aunt Mattie to hand the road map back to him, that he thought he could get us out of this mess. Uncle Pud was as mad as a wet hen because he was lost. George finally got us back to 19-41 Highway.

Then the worst thing happened! George's and my suitcase came loose and fell off the top of the car. An eighteen-wheeler truck ran over it, and our new clothes were all over the four-lane, except for one pair of my panties, which were caught on the grill of the eighteen-wheeler.

Aunt Mattie told Uncle Pud to just keep on driving. We screamed, "Stop the car! We have to have our clothes."

Uncle Pud pulled over to the side of the road and we picked up all of the clothes that were on the side of the road. When there was a break in the traffic, we got the few that we could out of the middle of the road. Clothes were flying everywhere! Cars were swerving to miss us, and nobody would help us.

George and I got most of our clothes back, wadded them up, and stuck them in the back seat of the car. Our new, expensive luggage was history.

Uncle Pud drove all night long, and we arrived in Panama City, Florida early the next morning. We were starving to death, but Aunt Mattie said we didn't have time to eat breakfast. We had to find a motel, so she told us to eat a cold biscuit.

George and I searched until we found our can of Vienna sausage. We pulled the key off the top of the can and opened it. We shared our sausages with Rodger, King, and Rose. Aunt Mattie told us to give Cupcake (who was growling) one. I told her that they were gone, as I stuffed the last one in my mouth. Cupcake nipped my hand and drew blood.

Aunt Mattie made Uncle Pud drive to about six motels. She went in every one of them and asked the price, and then we started looking again. She said that $15.00 was too much to pay for a room.

We finally came to the Come On Inn motel. A room there was $11.99. Aunt Mattie went in and got one room for all of us. George and I threw a fit. We were not about to sleep on the floor, and we had a pocket full of money.

Aunt Mattie wanted us to all stay in the same room so she could make us pay half the cost of the room.

We told her that we would get our own room. Aunt Mattie said that it "wouldn't be fittin'." We said that Rose could stay with us. Rose was the least obnoxious of their three children.

"George, you have a big ole zit right on the end of your nose," Rose said.

"It's not," I said. "It's a mosquito bite." Actually, it *was* a zit. George's face broke out every time he ate too much chocolate.

We toted armloads of clothes into our own pitiful room…and I do mean *pitiful!* There was torn linoleum on the floor, two beds with iron bedsteads, worn chenille bed spreads, a sink in the room, and a shower and toilet in the tiny bathroom.

I fell across a bed, and within ten minutes, I was fast asleep.

When I woke up, George was in the shower and Cupcake was in my bed with me. When I tried to get her off, she bit my hand again. Aunt Mattie and her obnoxious family was nowhere to be found.

I got up and tried to find my new pedal pushers. I couldn't find them…I thought they might still be in the middle of 19-41 Highway in Marietta, Georgia, so I put on my shorts and halter. George came out of the bathroom wearing his new madras shirt and new shorts.

We walked the three blocks to the ocean. I had never in my life seen or heard anything as beautiful as the ocean. I loved it!

We walked on the beach for awhile, minding our business. A smartass boy came up to George. "Hey big boy, did you get run over by a truck?"

George thought he was making fun of the zit on his nose. Since George had grown so much, and the incident with Wilson had happened, he wasn't willing to take a lot of shit. He could do a pretty good job of defending himself.

Just before George was about to flatten the boy, I noticed George's back. There was a big tire mark across the back of George's khaki shorts.

"Stop, George," I said. "He's serious. It *does* look like you were run over by a truck."

I told him about the tire mark on his shorts.

George said that maybe he could wash his shorts off in the ocean. We walked in, and George rubbed ocean water on the tire mark. It didn't help a bit. As a matter of fact, his new madras shirt started to bleed. The more George rubbed, the pinker George's shorts got.

Chapter 33

Back to Nashville

As we walked back to the Come On Inn Motel, it looked like George's legs were bleeding. That outfit was history!

We went in our room. At first, we thought somebody had broken in. Clothes were everywhere, and most of them had holes chewed in them.

"Cupcake!" we said at the same time. That hateful dog had ruined what was left of our clothes. We started picking them up and sorting them out. George had one pair of blue jeans and one T shirt that was alright. My straight skirt was fine.

We put Cupcake in Aunt Mattie's room and shut the door. Then, we went to the restaurant next door and ordered hamburgers, French fries, and Coke. That was the best food I have ever eaten in my life.

Aunt Mattie and her family came back with a grocery bag. They had bought a loaf of light bread and a jar of peanut butter.

"Mama said you can't eat our food," said Rodger. "We're having peanut butter sandwiches."

"We don't want your old supper," said George. "Alice Ivy and I just had a hamburger and some French fries."

"Cupcake tore up all our clothes," I said.

"She did not," said Aunt Mattie. "My sweetie wouldn't do that. Somebody must have broken in your room. I told you to make sure you locked your door."

"Her teeth marks are all over George's new blue suede shoes, and part of my shirt was hanging out of her mouth," I said.

"Say you're sorry, Cupcake. She didn't mean to," Aunt Mattie said.

"Mattie, the damn dog can't talk!" I said.

About that time, Rose came in with Cokes out of the Coke machine. She had on my new pedal pushers. I decided I wouldn't be mad at her. At least I had an outfit that had been saved from the wrath of Cupcake.

Poor Rose had awful clothes, homemade from feed sacks. Rose turned around to put the Cokes on the table, and I could see that the whole seat was busted out of my pedal pushers.

"Rose, why are you wearing my clothes?" I asked.

"Believe me, I don't know. These old cheap things, they are just no account," Rose said.

"Well, then take my cheap, no account clothes off, then, and never, and I do mean *never*, touch my clothes again," I said.

The next morning, I couldn't wait to see the ocean. I pinned up the hole in my bathing suit with a safety pin, and George pinned up the hole in his bathing suit. We headed for the beach. My beach hat was mashed flat somewhere along the side of the road in Georgia.

The ocean was even more beautiful than yesterday. We swam in the water, we walked on the beach, and we picked up sea shells. The sun was beaming down on us, really hot, but we didn't pay any attention to it, because there was a nice, cool breeze, too.

"Hey, Red, I believe you should get in the shade for awhile," said a rather cute boy.

"I'm fine," I said.

About three that afternoon I said, "I'm hungry. Let's go get something to eat." George agreed.

We went back to our tacky motel room and sorted through the rags Cupcake left us, trying to find something to wear. While we were looking for our clothes, it was starting to feel very hot. I had some bad thoughts about Aunt Mattie, because she didn't want to let us check into a motel with air conditioned rooms.

I put on my net can-can slip and the gathered skirt, and a shirt that didn't match. George got into his new blue jeans, and pulled on a shirt with a hole in it.

We went to the restaurant next door to get a bite to eat. When I sat down to order, I realized I was in enormous pain. Every part of my body was on fire.

The waitress came over to take our order.

"Honey, are you alright?" she asked.

"No, I think I'm going to die!" I wailed.

George wasn't any better off than I was. He was as red as a beet and shaking like a leaf.

"Honey, ya'll are blistered real bad," the kind waitress said, "I'm going to call your parents. What's the number?"

"It's long distance," I said.

"Where are ya'll from," she asked. "You look just like somebody I knew, from a long time ago." The waitress had tears in her eyes as she spoke to George.

"We're from Pea Ridge, Tennessee," I said.

"I used to live in Pea Ridge years ago. Well, I'll call your parents," the pretty waitress said.

We knew that Mama and Dr. Pooten were probably out of town. We thought Tibby might be at Dr. Pooten's, cleaning, so we gave the waitress Dr. Pooten's number. Sure enough, Tibby answered the phone. "Dr. Pooten;s residence."

The waitress explained the situation.

"Keep them there," said Tibby. "Give me your phone number."

In a few minutes, Dr. Pooten called. I got on the phone, and then the waitress talked with Dr. Pooten. She told him how bad George and I had gotten blistered.

"Get a taxi to the airport," Dr. Pooten told us. "I'll get your ticket from here and pick you up in Nashville."

It turned out that Mama and Dr. Pooten were already in Nashville. They had spent the night there.

I guess that was the day when I learned what money and power can do.

George and I had never flown in an airplane before. It was exciting, but we were too near death to enjoy the flight.

Dr. Pooten and Mama picked us up at the airport and drove us straight to the hospital. Mama would not speak to Aunt Mattie for a long time after that.

The poor waitress who helped us got chewed out by her boss. Before we left for the airport, we heard him cussing her, and she started to cry.

The next day, while we were in the hospital, we told Dr. Pooten all about how sweet the waitress was to us, and about how hateful her boss had been, and how he had cussed her out.

Dr. Pooten got on the phone and called the restaurant. He tried to explain to the boss what a nice thing the waitress had done, but the restaurant owner didn't want to hear about it. The waitress' boss cussed out Dr. Pooten. Dr. Pooten asked him to let him talk with the waitress.

It turned out that the waitress was a nurse who was down on her luck. Dr. Pooten hired her on the spot, provided she told her boss to take that job and shove it and then go straight to hell!

The nurse, Josie Tucker, turned out to be George's birth mother. She had found this out before we did, but she didn't want to be the one to tell us.

Mama had been getting money orders from her for years, and she had been putting them in George's college fund, but she never told us about this.

George and I already loved the waitress for saving our butts in Florida, so when the secret was exposed, the adjustment wasn't too hard on George.

He wanted to be mad at her for abandoning him when he was a baby. But after a short time, when we found out all the details about that, we all accepted Josie as part of our family.

Josie was fifteen years old when Old Dan caught his beautiful daughter in the back seat of Buck Hanks' car, fornicating. Old Dan shot Buck in the leg and sent Josie off to live with her aunt, the day after she gave birth to George. Old Dan got drunk after that, and he didn't sober up for the next sixteen years.

Chapter 34

Caught Somewhere Between Jesus and the Devil

By the time I got to college, I had friends who were girls, as well as George Washington. My roommates and I were as thick as molasses. We did everything together and we were always trying new things. This is what led up to George Washington's big drunk.

For the first couple of months of school, we had put more than one girl to bed and make her be quiet, because she had had too much to drink. Well, after all, we were grown now, and so we decided that we wanted to go out for a drink, too. I said that George Washington could drive us.

George said he would, and we made our plans. Our college was in a small town just outside of Nashville. We would go to Nashville to visit Ida, who had dropped out of school to become a model. Then, we would all go out for a drink, and George would be the driver.

Sometimes the best of plans go awry.

Everything went along just fine for a while. We went to a popular nightclub. At the last minute, Ida backed out, because she had a modelling job, but she told us how to get to the nightclub.

When we got there, the band was playing and people were dancing. We ordered Screwdrivers, and the waitress brought them over to our table. The first taste was awful, but after that, they tasted pretty good.

Like I've said before, George and I were good dancers. We got out on the dance floor, cutting a rug. Everybody moved back to give us room, and we really showed out!

The band took a break, and by this time we had finished our drinks, so we all ordered another. We were all happy!

We were hot from dancing, so we drank the second drink fast and ordered a third one. Just then, all hell broke loose! George came down with a bad case of religion! He was flinging his arms high in the air and preaching to everybody in the nightclub.

"This is a sin, this is a sin," he cried.

He got louder and louder, and people were looking at us.

"Shut up, George, please, please shut up!" I hissed.

Not only didn't George shut up, but he decided his sermon would have more power if he stood up on the table. The sermon was getting good, and I couldn't do anything with him.

"You harlots and whoremongers are all going to hell!"

He went on into his sermon about adultery and drunkenness. He started quoting the Bible. "And behold, there met him a woman with the attire of an harlot, and subtle of heart. Let not thine heart decline to her ways, nor go astray in her paths. For she hath cast down many wounded, yea, many strong men have been slain by her. Her house is the way to hell, going down to the chambers of death." (Prov. 7:10, 25-27)

People were there to have a good time…not to hear a hellfire and brimstone preacher, so the room started clearing out. The more I tried to make him be quiet, the louder he got.

The biggest bouncer I've ever seen came over and grabbed George, and pushed him through the room. Chairs fell over and George was still just a-preaching: "Repent, repent, you fools!"

The bouncer threw George right out the door.

The whole episode had been a sobering experience for me and my roommates, so we were in pretty good shape…we thought!

We piled preaching George in the car and put the top down so we could get some fresh air.

We started back to Ida's apartment. We drove and drove around Nashville, but we couldn't find it. We were hopelessly lost! Now, what were we going to do?

George started taking off his clothes and throwing them in the air. They were blowing everywhere. As he threw his clothes out, he quoted more scripture.

"It is easier for the camel to go through the eye of a needle than for a rich man to get into the Kingdom of Heaven."

"Lord, take my worldly possessions. Here's my shirt! Here's my pants!"

We screeched to a stop and started trying to find George's clothes. We got his pants back, but his shirt was too high on a tree limb to reach.

By this time, *I* had found religion. "Oh Lord, sweet Jesus," I prayed, "if you can find it in your heart to get this fool somewhere other than in jail or in a grave, I promise that whiskey will never touch my lips again! Amen."

The praying helped, because George let us put his britches on. Then, we saw a motel sign down the road.

"Lola, take your blouse off. I need it for George," I said.

"No!" Lola yelled.

"It'll calm him down. It's satin. Put your sweater on and button it up. It'll look just fine," I convinced her.

We got George's shoes on and put Lola's satin blouse on him. His hair was sticking straight up. The satin blouse with the ruffles down along the buttons didn't exactly fit. We pushed up the sleeves and tied it at the waist. We decided he could pass for a Spanish flamenco dancer. Now, to get to the motel and get him in the room. This wasn't going to be easy.

"How many of you?" asked the man behind the desk.

"Just us girls," we lied.

He gave us the key and we thought we had it made. We drove around to our room and George got out of the car.

About that time, the motel owner walked around the corner and saw us.

"He's a sick Spanish dancer," I tried to explain.

The motel owner was *so mad*. He shouted, "This is a decent establishment. We don't allow trash here. He's not sick…he's drunk! Now, get out of here and don't ever come back here!

We got George back in the car and started driving. Now, what were we gong to do? By this time, we were in the worst part of Nashville. We pulled into a seedy looking motel called *The Ritzy* and we made our plans.

We went into the motel and said we needed a room for five. The owner didn't care at all.

"Twenty dollars," he said.

We pooled our money and said, "We'll take it!"

Lola and I were the ones who went in the motel. We went back to get the others.

George was a sight! He had the fuzziest hair. When he was sober, he kept it very neat. Drunk was a different story. His fuzzy hair was sticking straight up, and he had on that satin blouse. His shoes were on the wrong feet.

We took him in the motel. "He's afflicted," I said.

The desk clerk didn't even raise an eyebrow. He kept looking down and counting our money.

We got George to the room and put him to bed.

"The room is spinning," he said. "Get on this bed, Alice Ivy…the bed's spinning."

"Put your foot on the floor," said Lola. "That'll stop the spinning."

Lola was wilder than George and me, and she had been drunk before.

The next morning, George was so hung over, he was just pitiful.

"I must have the flu," said George. "I think I'm going to die!"

"It's just a hangover," said Lola. "You'll be O. K. tomorrow."

George objected to wearing Lola's satin blouse with the ruffles down the front. I explained to him about him giving his clothes to Jesus, and he would have to go topless, or wear the blouse.

As we started out to get in our car, a drunk man and woman were just checking into a room.

"Hey, big boy, you must be some more stud," the man said, as he saw George with us four girls.

George balled up his fist to flatten the man, in the name of our somewhat tarnished reputation, but he stepped on his shoe string and stumbled into the drunk guy, knocking him for a loop.

The drunk got up, and when he saw how tall George was, he mumbled something about George not being able to take a joke. His girlfriend led him on into their room.

We had no money left. We were looking under the seats and in the glove compartment for some loose change. We found a stale, half-eaten Moon Pie and we each had a bite. That was our breakfast.

We headed back to the dorm when the unthinkable happened! Behind us was a car, with a blue light flashing and a siren wailing. We pulled over.

"Is your name George Washington Tucker Green?" a huge policeman asked George.

"Yes, sir," said George.

"You're under arrest," the policeman said.

"What can I do to help him?" I asked.

"Just come along peaceably. You're under arrest, too," said the policeman to the rest of us. "We've been looking for you all night. Your friend, Ida, called us and said you were missing. Follow me! We're going to the police station!"

"Please, please let us go," I begged. "We'll be good!"

"I'm calling your parents," the policeman said.

"Sir, they'll kill us," I cried.

"Ya'll should have thought of that before you got the entire Nashville police department looking for you. What's your phone number?"

Mama and Dr. Pooten arrived at the police station in about an hour. Dr. Pooten took a look at what George was wearing.

"What in the hell have you got on?" asked Dr. Pooten, who *never* cussed.

George hung his head in shame. I tried to lie to cover up what had really happened.

"George saw a beggar and gave him his shirt," I began.

"Shut up, Alice Ivy Green! You're lying through your teeth!" Mama would have no part of that.

I was thinking, "We're grown. They can't do much to us." Wrong! Wrong! Wrong!

"We'll see how you like walking," said Mama. "We'll give you enough money to eat for a month, and that's all!"

Then, Mama got on the phone and called Miss Raddle, our old maid dorm mother. She told Miss Raddle to "campus" us.

We cried as Mama drove away in our convertible.

The next month was pure hell. A coed can't possibly look as cute on foot as she does in a red convertible.

Miss Raddle took her job seriously. The only thing we could do during that month was to go to class and stay in our dorm room.

We all learned a valuable lesson from this experience: if you get hot while you're dancing, *drink water*!

Chapter 35

The End

George and Josie, his birth mother, became very good friends. Josie and Buck got married, and George said that made him a "son of a Buck."

Of all things, you won't believe this one. George now has a baby brother that looks just like him. He has a fitting name, too…Thomas Jefferson Hanks.

George graduated college with honors. As a matter of fact, he was third highest in his graduating class, and he blames me for not being number one. He said that if he hadn't gotten drunk and been so hung over, he would have made a higher grade on his chemistry test.

After college, George went to medical school and graduated fourth from the top. He couldn't blame me for not being number one this time!

George never was a big drinker, after his one and only big drunk.

After medical school, George went into practice with Mama's husband, Dr. John Pooten.

Mama finally figured out how to deal with Dr. Pooten's name. She kept her own name, but she used "Mrs. Pooten" when she wanted to impress people or when she needed money.

Mama June and Papa Jake sold the farm and moved to town. Mama June loves town as much as I do. She graduated college, the oldest in her class.

Aunt Martha completely lost her basket, but it doesn't matter, because she can still function just fine. She thinks she is the "Queen of Pea Ridge", and wears her crown and red cape most of the time. People in Pea Ridge treat her exactly the same, except the men give her a slight bow and the ladies curtsey when she passes by.

Aunt Mattie divorced Uncle Pud and married Abel Jones, the druggist. Abel said that if he couldn't marry Mama, he would just marry her sister. Aunt Mattie loves being married to Abel. He brings medicine home to her and listens to her about her ailments.

Wilson Gann became a holy roller preacher. My advice to him is to stay out of Mama's sight.

Big'un and Big'un's brother married sisters and bought a farm together. They raise the best beef and vegetables in the state of Tennessee. They also take very good care of their mother. And, they still turn white around the mouth at the mention of chocolate.

Dear, sweet Bucky drowned while trying to save Hessie's child.

Mabeline Lewis got a boob job.

I graduated from college, but not at the top of my class. I'm still finding myself, and I like most of what I find. I've had all kinds of jobs, but the truth is I just don't like hard work very much.

Life goes on pretty much as it always has in Pea Ridge, Tennessee.

978-0-595-38920-9
0-595-38920-1

Printed in the United States
63954LVS00005B/736-783